THE STOLEN NECKLACE

Dave Gustaveson

To
Lindsey
3-20-13

YWAM Publishing
A Ministry of Youth With A Mission

YWAM Publishing is the publishing ministry of Youth With A Mission. Youth With A Mission (YWAM) is an international missionary organization of Christians from many denominations dedicated to presenting Jesus Christ to this generation. To this end, YWAM has focused its efforts in three main areas: (1) training and equipping believers for their part in fulfilling the Great Commission (Matthew 28:19); (2) personal evangelism; (3) mercy ministry (medical and relief work).

For a free catalog of books and materials, contact:
YWAM Publishing
P.O. Box 55787, Seattle, WA 98155
(425) 771-1153 or (800) 922-2143
www.ywampublishing.com

The Stolen Necklace

Copyright © 1994 by David Gustaveson

13 12 11 10 09 08 07   11 10 9 8 7 6 5

Published by Youth With A Mission Publishing
P.O. Box 55787
Seattle, WA 98155

ISBN 0-927545-71-3

Printed in the United States of America.

To
Loren and Darlene
Cunningham,
and all the pioneers
who have followed since
the beginning of
Youth With A Mission
in 1960

Other

REEL KIDS
Adventures

Available at your local Christian bookstore or
through YWAM Publishing
1-800-922-2143
www.ywampublishing.com

Acknowledgments

There is something in our spirit that springs to life when we are challenged beyond ourselves. While researching for this book, I was amazed at the undying pioneer spirit of the missionaries who blazed the trails into East Africa.

These men and women looked at each obstacle as a stepping stone to victory. Nothing was impossible for them. In 1972, I was privileged to meet such a pioneer. I could see it in his eyes. Loren Cunningham had something I wanted. His pioneer spirit has marked Youth With A Mission and its growth.

I'm indebted to men like Loren. For years in YWAM, I've seen flames ignited in the hearts of kids as they have been presented with the challenge of world evangelism. My desire is to see thousands carry the torch of God's love.

This book is a way to spread the fire. Special thanks to Rod, Alexis, Psalm and Lael Wilson for their pioneer spirit and amazing stories of East Africa. Their help was special. Thanks to Dr. Dave Wilson for his insights and adventurous tour years ago through a national park in Africa.

Thanks to my friend John Davidson for his timely prayers. Thanks also to Tom Bragg, Warren

Walsh and Jim and Michelle Drake who are committed to publishing excellence. And I can't forget Jimmy Reyson who always lends computer skills.

And of course, special thanks to my editor, Shirley Walston, for her excitement over this project. her many hours of work are not unnoticed. Also to another children's author, Lois Johnson, for her timely encouragement along the way.

And to my dear mom who prayed for me in my dark years. Being a pioneer of the faith, she didn't give up on me.

And most important, I'm grateful to Jesus Christ, the greatest pioneer to ever walk this earth.

Table of Contents

Chapter 1

Danger in the Bush

Let's get out of here!"

Cold chills raced down 15-year-old Jeff Caldwell's spine. His muscles tensed. Combing his fingers nervously through his short blonde curls, he couldn't take his eyes off the gruesome scene. His skin tingled as he watched a trio of sand-colored lions rip at a helpless antelope.

"What if they come after us?" his younger sister Mindy whispered from the backseat.

"Would you cool it?" K.J. said casually. "We're inside a big ol' Jeep. We're safe, aren't we?"

The lions were almost as long as the Jeep—bigger than Jeff had ever imagined—and much too close for comfort. They were only thirty feet away.

Jeff looked at their guide, Ali, and waited for some kind of response to K.J.'s question. He didn't see any fear in Ali's eyes. He studied the guide's hawk-like profile and toffee-colored skin for a moment.

"What do you think, Ali?" he finally asked.

Ali smiled, showing the dark holes where his front teeth had been. "This Jeep is pretty strong. As long as those lions keep eating, we'll be okay."

One glance at Mindy showed Jeff how upset she was. Her hands covered her face as if she were watching a scary movie. Big brown eyes occasionally peeked through her fingers. When she began to pull at her blonde ponytail, Jeff knew trouble was near.

"Calm down, sis," Jeff said quietly. "We'll be okay."

"We've been here too long." Mindy's lip began to quiver. "I've seen enough animals for a lifetime. Let's go back to the lodge. It's safer there."

"Why did we bring along a 13-year-old girl, anyway?" Kyle James Baxter rolled his eyes. "Lions are what I came to Africa to see. This is terrific! We can't leave yet!" He shifted his video camera to his other shoulder.

Mindy groaned, pulling even harder on her ponytail.

Jeff shook his head, wondering if he would always have to play referee between his sister and his best friend. Their playful banter could at times get out of hand.

At that moment, one of the lions looked straight into K.J.'s camera lens. She casually licked her face before sticking it back inside the antelope.

"And you guys think I'm a messy eater!" K.J. laughed. "Look at those pigs!"

Jeff just grinned. He had known K.J. since the fifth grade. His best friend was crazy, impulsive, 14 years old, and had a thick crop of dark hair. Jeff loved K.J.'s ability to lighten up the most tense situations. A lot of energy was packed into his wiry 5'6" body.

K.J. winked and pulled down the brim of the Australian bush hat he thought made him look like an explorer. Mindy only groaned louder.

"Try to relax, Mindy," Ali said. "Lions in the park are not afraid of vehicles, only people. As long as we stay in the Jeep and don't startle them, they won't pay any attention to us. We need to leave soon anyway." He checked his watch. "Park rangers lock the gates at dusk, and it's almost five now. The old chaps will impose a fine if they catch us out after closing time. It's not safe here at night."

"Relax? How can I relax?" Mindy tried to control the panic in her voice. "K.J. and his camera always get us into trouble."

She turned to a laughing K.J. "I could kick you," she said, her teeth clenched.

"Not with those new desert boots you bought at the airport," K.J. pointed out. "They're more deadly than those lions!"

"What about yesterday, K.J.?" Mindy reminded him. "We'd barely arrived, and you made the witch doctor mad at us. And all because of your dumb camera."

"I don't think he liked us anyway," Jeff added quickly.

"Okay, okay. Truce," K.J. shouted. "I need to roll down the window so I can pick up the sound of lions licking their chops."

K.J. slowly rolled down the window, and everyone was startled by the terrible noise. The lions clawed at the antelope, tearing great chunks of meat away from the bones. Ripping their kill apart, they growled competitively.

The huge black-maned male got the choice pieces and the largest share. When one of the females got too close, he growled fiercely and swiped at her with a paw nearly as large as a baseball mitt.

The angry female got up, turned toward the Jeep, and crouched like she was ready to attack.

Instantly, K.J.'s camera dropped into his lap. He rolled the window up as fast as he could without startling her. An ear-deafening roar filled the Jeep, and the four of them jumped in unison, then ducked for cover. Mindy hid her face and curled deep into the seat. Everyone else covered their ears with their hands.

When Jeff didn't feel anything hit the car, he peeked out. The lion had repositioned herself and was chewing on another part of the antelope's body.

"I think it's okay," Jeff said with a sigh. "Looks like she went back to her dinner."

"Wow! Did you hear that?" K.J. cried when he looked up. "That was cool! I hope I got it on the tape."

"You mean *chilling*!" Mindy shot back. "Let's get out of here!"

Jeff waited for Ali to take charge. Though they had just met him the day before when he and their host, Mr. Salameh, had picked them up at the airport, they were beginning to feel like Ali was part of their group.

As Mr. Salameh's assistant, Ali's job was varied. This week, he was to guide his boss's Californian visitors. Jeff trusted him to make the safest decision.

"It gets dark quickly in Africa," Ali said, starting the engine. "We should head back to the lodge."

"I agree," Mindy chimed in. "I totally agree."

K.J. kept his trusty Canon Hi-8 camcorder running as they crept away from the scene. Jeff knew K.J. could never resist a photo opportunity like this one. Mindy watched as the lions disappeared from view.

After leaving the lions, the Jeep bounced down the dusty, rutted road. Jeff was excited to be in Tsavo East, one of Kenya's National Animal Reserves. In just a few hours they had seen giraffes, gazelle, and water buffalo—and that was before they ran into the lion kill. His eyes scanned the landscape, looking for more game.

Everyone got quiet as they moved down the road. Jeff could see that Mindy was beginning to relax.

"What are you thinkin' about, sis?" He turned in his seat to face her.

"I was trying to remember the name of our host. How do you remember everyone's names?"

"I associate the name with something," Jeff replied. "With Mr. Salameh, I think of salami. It sounds nearly the same."

"Jolly good way to think of him," Ali said, flashing his gums. They all laughed.

"I hope he and Warren were able to get us some meetings with those tribes," Mindy said. "It's too bad Warren couldn't come with us today. He always seems to miss all the adventure because he's busy with our arrangements. Being the leader must get boring."

"With all of his travels, we were certain Mr. Russell had seen animal reserves before," Ali said. "And Mr. Salameh has lived in Africa all his life. Besides, they were scheduling appointments for you."

At the word "scheduling," Jeff chuckled to himself. He had been surprised to find English such a common language in Kenya—even if it was the British-English that pronounced scheduling "shed-yul-ing." And Ali's lack of teeth made some words sound even more funny. Jeff always had to listen carefully.

"I still wish Warren were here," Mindy said. "As scary as it was to be so close to those lions, it *was* an incredible experience. I can't wait to get to my laptop to write the video script."

"Tell me about your club," Ali asked as they rode along. "What is it you do with videos?"

"We're called the 'Reel Kids,'" Jeff began, thrilled for the opportunity to talk about his favorite subject. "Warren Russell is our teacher—and our friend, too. He started the club a few years ago at our school, Baldwin Heights High School, which is in the Los Angeles area."

"What is the purpose?" Ali wanted to know.

"It was started to take students on field trips to other countries," Jeff replied. "Warren is the head of the Communications Department. The club allows us to practice our skills while we travel.

"K.J. is our cameraman, and Mindy does the research and writes video scripts. I speak to groups and try to keep these two in line when Warren is busy. We meet off campus, but we're able to use school equipment."

"What made you want to study communications?" Ali seemed to be genuinely interested.

"I guess it's in the genes." Jeff smiled. "My dad is an anchorman on a local television station, and my mom works part-time as a news correspondent. 'Reel Kids' produces videos to challenge other teenagers like us at the churches in our area. We hope to inspire them to send teams of their own to the nations we visit."

"Why are you called 'Reel Kids?'" Ali asked as he turned sharply onto a smaller dirt road.

Jeff started to answer when he noticed a sudden look of terror on Ali's face. Ali jammed on the brakes and a thick dust cloud surrounded the Jeep. They couldn't see a thing—only gray.

"What's wrong?" Jeff asked.

"What happened?" Mindy added, leaning into the front seat.

"Didn't you see the elephants?" he asked. Ali was shocked. "How could you miss a herd of elephants? We almost ran into one. They're right in the middle of the road!"

Mindy gasped. K.J. reached for his camera.

"Why don't we turn around?" Jeff said.

"I took this old road because it's a shortcut to the lodge." For the first time since their trip had begun,

Ali sounded nervous. "If we turn around now, we'll have to go back the way we came and take the long way back."

"What's wrong with that?" Jeff pressed.

"Time. It'll take an hour." Ali sighed. "Darkness comes quickly on the plains. We will not get back in time, which means trouble with the rangers."

"What do we do now?" Mindy wondered.

"Don't do anything yet!" K.J. yelled. "This settling dust is terrific. I'm getting an incredible shot of elephants appearing out of nowhere. There must be 15 of them!"

"We'll have to wait a spell," Ali said. "Hopefully they will move off the road. I don't dare try driving through them because some could get behind us. We don't want to be in the middle of an elephant herd. At eight tons, they have tremendous strength and could easily roll the Jeep over. They've been known to drive their tusks through the sides of cars."

No one said a word.

K.J. filmed the impressive herd. Mindy's eyes became as big as the frames of her glasses, but Jeff was more focused on the elephants than his sister at the moment.

Ali kept the motor running and tried to distract the group by launching into his tour-guide routine.

"Elephants are amazing animals," he began. "They can stand 11 feet at the shoulder and eat 400 pounds of twigs, grass, leaves, and bark every day."

"That's right! They don't eat meat," Mindy interrupted, always looking for a chance to share her research. "They live in matriarchal societies. Females spend their whole lives with their mother's family.

The males leave the herd as adolescents and travel with another male or two."

"They drink about 50 gallons of water at a time," Ali added. "These are females. Adult males are nearly twice this size. Because their tusks are extremely valuable, they are in danger. Kenya has a problem with poachers who kill them, cut off their ivory tusks, and leave their magnificent bodies to rot. It's a horrible—" he paused, his eyes growing wide. "Oh, my. Here they come."

Ali cautiously shifted into reverse and backed the Jeep around the turn. He put the car back in neutral and sat, waiting for the road to clear. Unfortunately, the elephants followed them around the curve.

"Will they hurt us?" Mindy asked.

"They certainly could if they decided to charge," Ali replied. "I say. I could I tell you some jungle stories!"

"No thank you!" Mindy exclaimed. "Not now."

Massive gray bodies trudged toward the Jeep. Jeff had seen elephants in the zoo, but out the window of the Jeep they looked more like a wrinkled gray wall. Their giant tusks were pointed at the group like lethal weapons. The elephants' shrieking roars grew louder.

"Look. There's a couple of babies hidden behind their mothers," K.J. said, straining to get a better shot.

"That could be even more dangerous." Ali's eyes looked glassy; his face tightened in fear. "They are very protective of their young. Let's wait a few more minutes."

"We should have gone the other way," Mindy said.

"Relax," Jeff pleaded. "He knows what he's doing."

"I've taken this shortcut before. It cuts 45 minutes off our return."

Jeff wiped beads of sweat from his upper lip. He knew it was time to pray, and pray hard.

"Let's pray that God would move them off the road."

"You pray," Mindy urged.

Jeff couldn't seem to close his eyes, but the words began to roll off his lips.

"Lord, you made the world, and you created these elephants. Please send them the other way and make a path for us to get back to the lodge."

Everyone said "Amen" in unison.

Jeff knew the elephants were much too close. Though they weren't charging, he was still nervous. Why wasn't God answering his prayer?

Suddenly there was a hissing noise. Everyone looked around when they heard it.

"It's coming from the Jeep!" K.J. cried.

"Oh no," Ali moaned. "The engine is heating up."

"What now?" Jeff asked in frustration, seeing steam roll out from under the hood. He looked at the temperature gauge—the needle was rising. "We'd better do something or the radiator will boil over!"

"We'll have to go up the road," Ali said, "and park long enough to let it cool."

The team sat in silence as Ali turned the Jeep around the way they had come. Driving slowly, they went a mile up the road.

"At least we're a mile further from the elephants," K.J. pointed out, always trying to find a bright spot in every situation.

Ali reached down to shut off the motor, but the engine quit before he touched the key. Everyone looked at each other in concern.

Jeff checked the gauge again. It was still hot. The hissing was getting on his nerves. Steam continued to pour out from under the hood. He prayed desperately. The club loved adventure, but this was a little too close to the edge.

"Africa!" he grumbled to himself. He had dreamed for months of making the summer trip, but now he almost wished he hadn't come. Jeff thought Ali would know what to do, but he seemed nearly as frightened as the kids. Minutes passed too slowly as they waited for the engine to cool.

K.J. picked up his camera again and stuck it in Mindy's face.

"This is a good time for an on-the-spot interview," he said in his best TV interviewer voice. "I'm going to ask you a few questions." Turning to Jeff, he whispered, "This will make great footage."

Mindy pushed the camera away. "Stop it, K.J. This is not the time to be funny."

"It's better than being with that witch doctor," K.J. said.

"You're right about that. Why do you think he got so mad at us?" Mindy asked.

"It sure wasn't a very nice way to welcome us to Kenya," Jeff said.

"The only advice I can offer you, K.J., is to use caution with that camera." Ali shook his head and smiled. "Villagers don't appreciate being filmed without permission."

"I shouldn't have to get a witch doctor's permission," K.J. protested. "They're not supposed to be afraid of anything."

"Never mind," Jeff said. "Let's be careful from now on."

The hissing and steaming of the engine slowed slightly. Jeff looked over his shoulder. The elephants were disappearing into a group of large trees on the side of the road.

K.J. reached into his pocket and held up a shiny green stone the size of his fingernail.

"Look what I found last night in the village," he said.

They passed around the beautiful gem and studied it. For a moment the four of them were distracted from the dangers of elephants and getting stuck in the park at night.

"I say," Ali reached for the stone, "it looks like an emerald. Look at the carving on it. Where did you say you found it?"

As K.J. opened his mouth to answer, Mindy gasped. Jeff turned to see why. The elephants were no longer eating leaves off the large trees. Now they were coming straight at the Jeep!

"What should we do?" Mindy cried.

"I'll start the Jeep and get us out of here," Ali yelled.

They all held their breath while Ali turned the key. But instead of the sound of an engine starting, they heard grinding noises. Ali tried again. And again. Over and over. Nothing.

"The battery is nearly dead." Ali kicked the floor with his big leather boots. "If it does, we'll never get out of here tonight."

Silently, Jeff talked to God.

Ali tried again.

Mindy shouted, "Yes!" when the engine finally roared to life. The elephants were just yards away.

Everyone held their breath as Ali backed up. They were getting to know this section of road well. Too well.

"I think we'll try the long way," Ali said. "At this point, the authorities seem less dangerous than the elephants."

"Fine with us," Jeff agreed.

Ali backed further away from the oncoming herd until he found a wide spot in the road. He turned the Jeep around toward the main road, and everyone cheered.

As they made themselves comfortable for the long journey, they laughed about their incredible day.

Suddenly, three elephants wandered out from behind the trees. Jeff couldn't believe his eyes. Their gigantic size and enormous tusks told him they must be males. They trotted straight at the Jeep. He heard K.J. pull out his camcorder and stick it out the window. Jeff looked around for a way of escape. Nothing.

"Here comes the Elephant Cavalry," K.J. said. "Those females must have called them with all their noise."

"More elephants! I'm not certain where they have all come from today," Ali said, shaking his head. "The trees are too thick to enable us to pass. And I can't back up because the other herd is behind us."

"We're trapped!" Mindy cried.

Chapter 2

Too Late

Jeff turned to Ali. "I thought animal parks were safe!" he said.

"They are. At least in the daytime." Ali shrugged helplessly. "Remember, this is the time of day when the animals are out looking for dinner. We should have been out of here by now. This wouldn't have happened if I'd gotten back on the main road after we saw the lions."

"This looks serious even to me," K.J. said. "What's the plan?"

"First, I'll have to turn the engine off again. It'll

get hotter if it idles," Ali said. "Just keep low and be still."

"You mean we're going to stay here?" Mindy asked, her eyes wide.

"I suppose you have a better idea?" K.J. quipped.

"We have no other choice," Ali said. "With any luck, they will walk right past us."

"I don't think they like us on their turf," K.J. said, adjusting his lens.

Jeff turned around to see what the first herd was doing. He did a doubletake when he saw them, still nearly a mile away, heading toward the Jeep! He felt the road closing in.

"Do you think they'll attack?" Mindy asked.

"Here's the way to tell." Ali was watching the elephants closely. "If they hold their ears out wide, it's a fake charge. If they put their ears back, we could be in a speck of trouble."

"What do you mean?" Mindy began to pull on her ponytail.

"When they mean business, their ears lie flat against their shoulders and they tuck their trunk between their front legs," Ali said.

"What will happen if they charge us?" Mindy pressed.

K.J. groaned at her. "Mindy, it means we're dead meat."

"Before a charge they get into a slight crouch," Ali added.

"I don't think I can take this," Mindy cried.

"Shhh," Ali demanded. "Get down in your seats. They're getting closer. We don't want to give them any cause for anger."

Everyone got down on the Jeep floor. K.J. held his camera above his head to shoot whatever was happening out the window.

Jeff's thoughts raced wildly. His African dream was turning into a nightmare. They were about to be attacked by elephants! Who would ever believe this?

As the elephants got closer, their shrieks and trumpeting sounds became deafening.

Jeff felt his trembling muscles tighten, then he prayed quietly.

"Where are they?" Mindy asked.

"Shhh," Ali demanded.

"Can't they smell us?" K.J. asked quietly.

"Shhh," Ali whispered forcefully.

Jeff saw a large tusk just inches from the Jeep, like a giant sword against the darkening blue sky.

A large elephant's eye peered in at them.

"He's looking right at us!" K.J. cried in a frightened whisper.

Everyone felt the large thud at once. Then a jerk.

"He's trying to turn the Jeep over!" Mindy said in a hushed panic.

Jeff couldn't believe his eyes. Leathery gray skin surrounded the Jeep, towering over it.

"Maybe we could make a run for it!" K.J. suggested.

"No!" Ali said. "There is nowhere to run. And there are other wild animals out there who'd love to have a nice dinner."

"Don't say that!" Mindy gasped.

The right front tire of the Jeep came slightly off the ground. Jeff expected a tusk to crash through a window or pierce the radiator.

Jerk. Jerk. Thud. Jerk.

"I think they're just playing." Ali laughed nervously. "If we lay perfectly still, they might leave us alone and go on their way."

"This is playing?" Mindy questioned.

"I hope so," Ali replied weakly.

"It's getting dark," K.J. said. "I want to get some good footage of this, especially if this is my last video shoot."

Everyone was too frightened to argue. K.J. sat up to adjust his camera. The sound of the camcorder reel was muffled by the elephant cries. The bumps and jerks were steady.

Suddenly, Jeff felt the front end of the Jeep lift at least a foot off the ground.

Mindy stifled a scream. K.J. dropped his camera.

"Don't move," Ali ordered. "Lying still is our only hope. And be quiet!"

The jerking got worse. The shrieks and cries of the elephants were terrifying. The thuds became more violent.

Jeff peeked through the seats. K.J. looked as terrified as Mindy.

"Ali," Jeff cried in a whisper. "I don't know if you believe in prayer, but God is the only one who can save us."

Stirring up all his faith, Jeff began, "Lord Jesus, you alone can stop those elephants from hurting us. We're on a mission for you, and in Jesus' name we stand against the powers of darkness that would want to stop us."

Instantly, the jerking stopped. The Jeep fell to the ground with a giant thud, then bounced to a stop. No one said a word as they pulled themselves up to peek out the windows.

They gasped in relief. Jeff was amazed to see the elephant hurrying away—with his ears still back. Jeff held his breath and kept praying as the angry beast raced across the road in full charge.

Everyone watched in awe and total disbelief.

"What happened?" Mindy finally asked.

"He took off into the trees," Jeff said. "I have no idea why."

"I don't believe in your God," Ali said, "but I think your prayer was answered. Let's take advantage of the elephant's hasty retreat."

Ali tried to start the engine, but the grinding starter just whined.

"Come on, baby," K.J. cried. "You can do it."

Everyone cheered when the engine roared to life. Ali put the Jeep in gear and slowly pulled away. They drove past two more elephants, but the beasts were busy peeling the bark off of trees.

As the Jeep inched down the road, Jeff looked around and realized how dark the night was becoming. He knew Ali couldn't turn on the headlights until they were completely out of danger, though.

Finally, as the Jeep crept past the last elephant, everyone let out a big sigh of relief. They all knew God had answered their prayers.

"I'm glad that's over," Mindy moaned.

"It's not over yet," Ali replied. "We still have to get back to the lodge. I could use more of those prayers."

"What should we pray for?" Jeff asked.

Ali looked over, his face wet with perspiration.

"That we don't encounter any more elephants— or anything else for that matter!"

Jeff, Mindy, and K.J. each prayed. Then everyone grew quiet. It seemed like an eternity had passed since they left the compound that morning.

As they rode along, they caught occasional glimpses of giraffes and elephants in the beam of the headlights, but none were close enough to worry about. When the road widened, Ali broke the silence.

"I think we're safe now," he announced. "This road is much better. Perhaps you could tell me more about your club. You seem very religious."

"We don't consider it religious," Jeff said. "The people in the club have a personal relationship with God."

"What do you mean by a personal relationship with God?" Ali asked suspiciously. "I've always lived along the coast lands, and most people are Muslims like me. Christians have tried to tell me about this, but I still don't believe it's possible to know God personally."

"It's a relationship where God becomes your best friend," Jeff explained. "Just like when I prayed out there. God loves to answer the prayers of his people."

"Well," Ali replied, "he jolly well took his time."

"Sometimes." Jeff grinned. "But he always comes through. That's what makes our club so exciting. God is not some boring person. He makes our lives filled with adventure."

"You mean this is not unusual for you?" Ali laughed.

"Well, elephants, yes." Jeff laughed with him.

"But when we go out on trips for Him, we often run into trouble."

"Trouble from the devil?" Ali probed.

"Well, yes," Jeff answered.

"In Kenya, some people follow witch doctors." Ali grew serious. "They call on evil spirits and sometimes put curses on people."

"But there is a greater power than any evil spirit," Jeff pointed out. "It's the power of Jesus Christ."

"If that is the power that moved those elephants, I'd like to learn more about it," Ali said.

"Sure." Jeff grinned even bigger. "Sure."

"Hey! We're at the park gates!" K.J. yelled as bright lights came into view. "That must be the lodge."

"Wow!" Mindy exclaimed. "Is that a happy sight, or what?"

"Yeah. I don't remember it looking this good when we dropped off our bags this morning," K.J. said.

Ali drove up to the security building. The gates were closed and locked.

Jeff noticed the look on the security guard's face as he stomped up to the Jeep. He was not happy. He took his time walking around the Jeep, peering in the windows and under the vehicle with his flashlight. Stopping at the driver's side, he shined the beam in each of their faces.

"You are a local," he said to Ali. "Don't you know the rules around here?"

"Yes, sir."

"Then why are you late?"

"We were delayed on the road by elephants," Ali replied.

"You were off the main road, weren't you?"

"Yes, sir," Ali said. "We tried the shortcut."

"I thought so," he said, shaking his head. "Don't you know there is a fine for being in the park this late?"

"Yes, sir."

"Get out of the Jeep," he snapped. "You're all in trouble."

Chapter 3

The Stolen Necklace

I'm starved," K.J. complained as he followed Jeff and the others to the security office. "What's the big deal, anyway? So we're a little late."

"Shhh," Ali whispered. "I recommend letting me do the talking. You might get a free meal and a room if you're not careful," he added quietly.

Just before entering the little office, Jeff glanced back toward the Jeep and noticed a dent in the door, right in the "Mombasa Tea Company" sign.

"Uh, oh," he mumbled under his breath, "Mr. Salameh is not going to be very happy when he sees that dent." He wondered what else could possibly go wrong.

The security guard pointed to some wooden chairs, and one by one the four of them plopped down to face the angry man.

"Don't you know how dangerous it is after dark on those roads?" the guard asked. "Our rules are for your own safety. It is forbidden to be in the park this late."

Jeff, Mindy, and K.J. waited for Ali to answer.

"It's my fault, sir," Ali admitted. "I made the mistake of getting off into the bush."

The guard ignored Ali's comment and turned to K.J.

"What is your purpose in our country?"

"We're here to do some research," K.J. replied. "And we're also doing a video for our club in America."

"What club is this?"

"A communications club called the 'Reel Kids.'"

"I hope someone has informed you about not taking pictures of the locals," the guard said angrily. "Film the animals all you want, but it is impolite to take photos of people without permission."

"Yes, sir," K.J. said.

The guard turned toward Ali. "My job is to protect people. That was a foolish thing you did. Tourists don't understand, but you know Kenya. You know better."

"Yes, sir," Ali replied, hanging his head.

"I'm going to let you off this time, but I'll remember you. If this ever happens again, you'll pay the maximum fine."

Ali thanked the guard, and the four of them hurried back to the Jeep before he could change his mind.

Once inside, K.J. was the first to speak.

"Are the guards always that tough on tourists?" he asked Ali.

"They're strict about the rules," Ali said. "That's their job, but he softened up."

"Let's get to our rooms," Mindy said. "I can't wait to take a shower."

"And eat," K.J. said.

"I'll second that," Jeff agreed.

Within minutes the group was standing in the lobby of the lodge. Through a wall of windows they could see a watering hole as big as an Olympic-sized pool. At night floodlights lit the area so those staying at the lodge could watch animals come to drink. Salt licks had been added to attract wild game.

Walking through the spacious room, the group was surrounded by lions, tigers, giraffes, and elephants—some stuffed and hanging on the walls, some peering down from paintings and photos.

They quickly found their rooms. Jeff and K.J. were sharing a room that had two full-size beds. Mindy felt like a queen because she got a big room all to herself.

As everyone met in the hallway a few minutes later, a porter appeared with a note.

"Look," Mindy said. "A message for us?"

Jeff reached for the note and thanked the porter. He opened the folded piece of paper. K.J. glanced over Jeff's shoulder.

"It's from Warren and Mr. Salameh," K.J. said, spotting the names at the bottom.

Jeff pulled the note closer.

"Warren wants us back at Likoni first thing in the morning," he said. "Something has come up. He'll explain then."

"That's kind of weird," K.J. said. "But it won't do us any good to worry about it now. I'm hungry enough to eat one of those elephants!"

The sun's blazing rays awakened everyone early Monday morning. Mindy's guidebooks had said the temperatures would be only around 80 degrees in July, but they all woke up sweltering in the tropical sun.

Jeff hadn't slept very well. He was worried about Warren's message. He knew it must be serious if Warren asked them to come back early. Jeff sighed and did what he could to hurry Mindy and K.J. as they packed up.

On the journey back to Likoni, they talked mostly about God. K.J. and Mindy leaned forward the whole way, helping Jeff answer Ali's questions. The lively discussion made the trip go by quickly

Mr. Salameh's house was located in Likoni, on the outskirts south of Mombasa. Jeff was thankful they'd been invited to stay there, especially since the property bordered on a small village that would be perfect for filming Kenya's tribal life.

Jeff saw Mr. Salameh relaxing on the lawn when they drove into the driveway. Behind Mr. Salameh was a two-story house that had a balcony overlooking the yard. Under it were white pillars and a wrap-around porch scattered with hammocks and wicker chairs. French doors stood open like welcoming arms. Three smaller buildings were set to the back of the large property. Jeff wondered why the windows were covered with bars.

"I'm glad you guys are here!" Warren called as he walked up the driveway toward them.

Climbing out of the Jeep, Jeff realized how happy he was to see Warren. Away from school, they called their leader by his first name. Even though Warren was in his early thirties, he was sometimes mistaken for a student. K.J had called him "Capt'n Warren" on the plane because his latest haircut made him look like an Army recruit.

Warren had a medium build and was only an inch taller than Jeff. As usual, he wore jeans, but because of the heat, he had on a polo shirt instead of his usual sweater. Ponytail flying, Mindy ran to tell Warren all about yesterday's adventures.

As Ali helped unload their bags, Mr. Salameh came over to greet them. He was over six feet tall, slim, and a native Kenyan. His neatly pressed white shirt, tan suit, and polished leather shoes made Jeff decide he was a successful businessman with the Mombasa Tea Company.

Mr. Salameh had large eyes and a dignified face. Dark-framed glasses were nearly invisible against his skin, which was the color of deep, rich chocolate.

Even before they met, Jeff had been impressed with Mr. Salameh. A friend of Warren's had recommended they call him when they began praying about this trip. He explained that Mr. Salameh was Swahili, part of Kenya's royal lineage. He had been raised a Muslim but ever since he heard about Jesus, he made time from his busy schedule to share his faith with surrounding tribes.

Jeff and Warren had been thrilled when they contacted him. Mr. Salameh had generously offered to help in any way he could, inviting the team to stay at his house and lending them his assistant, Ali, as their guide.

Everyone talked at once. Mindy and K.J. were telling their frightening lion and elephant stories to Warren. Jeff recognized the look in Warren's eyes and knew Warren wished he could have come with them instead of staying at the house to finalize their plans.

Jeff laughed, listening to Mindy describe their narrow escape. She sounded so brave now. When Mindy finally took a breath, Jeff jumped into the conversation.

"So why did you want us here so early? What's up?" he asked. Warren's face became serious.

"A problem came up in the village where we filmed the night we arrived," he said.

Mindy leaned in expectantly.

"The witch doctor who gave us trouble there is telling everyone that his expensive necklace has been stolen," Warren added.

"What's that got to do with us?" Mindy asked.

Mr. Salameh frowned at her. "He's telling everyone that you took it. He has a lot of power with the people, and it will not make it easy on your mission."

"What kind of necklace was it?" Jeff asked, puzzled.

"Gold, set with specially carved emeralds."

K.J. reached slowly into his jeans pocket and pulled out the sparkling green stone. "Do you think this was part of it?"

Everyone stared at K.J.

"Why are you all looking at me?" K.J. asked, taking a step backwards.

"Where did you get that?" Mr. Salameh asked.

"I found it near the village."

"You're going to have to prove that." Mr. Salameh looked very concerned. "The witch doctor says he saw one of you near his hut."

"I was doing some filming when the light from my camera hit something sparkling on the ground," K.J. said. "I reached for it and found this stone."

"Well, I don't know if he'll believe that," Warren sighed. "He seemed awfully upset."

"He's coming here this morning at ten," Mr. Salameh said, "and bringing the police with him."

"This is most unusual," Ali observed. "Witch doctors don't wear necklaces. It must be something special."

"I got the impression he doesn't like us," Mindy said. "He wasn't very friendly when we first arrived."

"Well, he'll be here in a half-hour," Warren said. "Let's hope we can straighten this out."

"I guess we'll just have to wait, then." Jeff paused. "By the way, were you able to set up any meetings for us?"

"Yes," Mr. Salameh replied. "You'll visit with the Masai tribe tomorrow afternoon. The chief is interested in meeting you and seeing the film you brought."

"That's great!" Mindy exclaimed.

Jeff looked over at Warren, who was now sitting down.

"You don't look so good, Warren," Jeff said. "Did you get enough sleep last night?"

"I'm still jet-lagged from the trip," Warren admitted. "I think the time change is getting to me. I'm going to go lie down while you guys get settled."

Ali helped carry the kids' bags into the house.

They walked through a large living room that had a zebra rug in front of the fireplace and photos of wild game on the walls. Stairs to the left led to the spacious second story, where Mr. Salameh and his wife's rooms were. They hadn't met Mrs. Salameh; she was away on a trip.

Mindy was shown to a guest room on the first floor. Just like in the movies, there was a tent of mosquito netting over the bed. She couldn't resist plopping on the mattress, just for a second.

K.J. and Jeff were taken to a guest cottage right outside the kitchen door. "Hey, this is going to be all right!" K.J. poked Jeff in the ribs. The servants quarters were located not far away in the back, where Ali and the other helpers lived.

While they were unpacking, a commotion outside made Jeff look out one of the guest cottage's screened windows. The village was so close, he could see dozens of huts. Most of the tribal people were busy with their daily duties.

The noise was coming from a small crowd of people heading toward the house. The witch doctor led the group. A uniformed man, who was probably the village policeman, walked beside him. The crowd looked serious.

Jeff and K.J. ran to get Warren out of a hammock on the porch. He looked a little dazed as he rose from his nap, and Jeff noticed beads of sweat on his face.

Mindy, Ali, and Mr. Salameh quickly joined the others in the yard.

The witch doctor walked up and pointed a bony finger at them.

"Those foreigners are the ones who stole my necklace," he accused.

Jeff tried to remain calm. He didn't want to show how afraid he was, but he saw the power the witch doctor had over the people. They hung on his every word.

Jeff studied him. He was shorter than Mindy and couldn't have weighed more than a hundred and twenty pounds. He walked with a limp and had a carved wooden cane. Jeff guessed the witch doctor was about forty years old.

Barechested and barefooted, he stood out from the people by wearing a black kanga cloth knotted around his waist. Many people wore kangas, Mindy had told them earlier, but only the witch doctor wore black. An assortment of amulets and leather pouches hung around his wrists and neck, probably containing the Muslim prayers and powders Mindy had also mentioned.

The witch doctor had a prominent nose and his beard ran along his chin line. His skin was lighter than many of the others. But it was the evil look in those dark, piercing eyes that caught Jeff's attention.

"I've talked to everyone, and they've assured me that they didn't take your necklace," Warren said.

"You're lying." The witch doctor pointed toward K.J. "Someone saw your friend near my hut."

K.J. took a step back. His face turned pale.

Warren walked right up to the witch doctor. Jeff had always respected Warren's boldness and knew he would take charge. Though today Warren didn't look so good. He was sweating from the heat.

"I have questioned K.J. about this," Warren said calmly. "He has convinced me that he didn't take your necklace."

"I know he is guilty," the witch doctor insisted. "That necklace is a rare treasure I purchased on the island of Zanzibar. I want it back. Now."

Warren turned to K.J. and asked for the stone. K.J. dug it out of his pocket and handed it to Warren, who held it up for the witch doctor to see.

"Is this part of your missing necklace?"

At the sight of the emerald, the witch doctor's eyes narrowed and his face filled with anger, then rage.

"I knew it! What did you do with the rest of it?"

"K.J. found it on the ground near your village," Warren said. "This one stone was lying in the dirt. He had no idea it was yours."

"You're lying!" the witch doctor yelled. "You'll live with a curse on your lives because of this."

K.J. walked over to Warren and took the emerald. He quickly handed it to the witch doctor.

"Here. I didn't take your necklace. Everything Warren has told you is true. I'm not a thief."

The witch doctor studied the emerald, then turned to the policeman.

"He's lying. He stole my necklace! Arrest him immediately."

Chapter 4

Mysterious Fever

The policeman rushed over and grabbed K.J.'s arm, and Jeff realized that the witch doctor had more power over these people than he had thought. Even the policeman was scared of him.

He knew the policeman didn't have any evidence against K.J., but he wondered what would happen next. Even with all of Mindy's research, he knew nothing about Kenya's jails or legal system.

"I'm taking him to police headquarters," the policeman said to Warren. "He had one of the emeralds on him, and he needs to answer some more questions."

K.J. started to pull away, but Warren put a comforting arm on his shoulder.

"It'll be okay, K.J.," Warren said quietly. "We'll go with you. You did nothing wrong."

Jeff was relieved when his hot-headed friend nodded to the policeman and followed peacefully.

Mr. Salameh motioned for Ali to get the Jeep. Warren joined K.J. in the police Land Rover while Jeff and Mindy rode the short distance with Ali.

Even though the situation was tense, Jeff couldn't help laughing as they passed a family of screaming brown baboons playing alongside the road.

"They're playing like kids on a playground!" Mindy squealed in delight. "And look at that one, Jeff! His face looks like Luke—you know, our neighbor's dog."

The large males chased each other through tree branches, and tiny babies clung to the undersides of their mothers. Jeff was fascinated. The baboons chattered loudly to one another. Their long, sharp fangs surprised him.

"Are they dangerous?" he asked Ali.

"They're very strong—much bigger and stronger than their monkey cousins." Ali grinned. "Mostly they're just pesky little chaps who eat from our fruit trees or take things left in the yard. But if they are provoked, they are strong enough to tear someone to bits."

"Hey!" Mindy said with a sly look. "Do you think we could introduce them to the witch doctor?"

Jeff gave her a disapproving glance. "Mindy..." he said sternly.

"I know, I know, we should love our enemies. Anyway," Mindy said, "researching Africa was fun, but actually being here is sure different—and more dangerous—than I thought."

"It's not that bad," Ali replied. "Tourists rarely get hurt. I'm sorry about taking the wrong road last night. Kenya is such a beautiful place that I wanted to show it to you. I think I scared you instead."

"We forgive you, Ali." Mindy patted his shoulder.

"We seem to find excitement wherever we go," Jeff added, grinning.

Ali laughed.

They soon pulled up to the police station, which was surrounded by a twelve-foot cyclone fence. The square building was made of whitewashed coral rock and probably used to look nice, Jeff decided. Now the walls were caked with dirt.

When Warren motioned to them, they quietly filed inside. As Jeff walked in, he noticed the simple furnishings—an office desk, a chair, a file cabinet, and a telephone. The lone, bare, hanging lightbulb offered only a little light.

Muffled voices could be heard from behind one of the two closed doors. That probably meant prison cells were behind the other. Jeff shuddered at the thought of his best friend being locked up in this dismal place.

"It's hot in here," Jeff said while they waited.

"This is one of the hottest Julys we've had in five years," Ali said. "We could really use some rain. This drought is causing serious water problems."

"It sure is taking its toll on me," Warren replied.

"You don't look so good, Capt'n," K.J. said.

"Don't worry about me. We need to clear up this whole mess first."

"What do you think, Ali?" Jeff asked.

"The witch doctor is trying to destroy your reputation with the people," Ali said. "If he can keep people away from outsiders, he stays in control."

A man they had never seen before stepped into the room. He wore khaki shorts and shirt, a black tie, and boots that came halfway to his knees. Although he wore no badge, his erect posture and official-looking patches on his sleeves indicated he was in charge.

He sat at the desk and took his time looking over the papers he had pulled from a file folder. The whole group shifted from foot to foot while they waited.

Finally, the officer looked up. "I'm the police chief for this district. I understand one of you is accused of stealing jewelry from Mohammed Abdul."

Jeff heard the witch doctor's name for the first time.

K.J. stepped forward. "I found a stone in a field," he said. "He says it's from his necklace."

The chief's eyes went back to his paperwork. "These charges against you come from the most powerful man in our village," he pointed out. "It would be wise to cooperate."

"We're here to cooperate," Warren replied.

"Who are you?"

"I'm Warren Russell, leader of this group."

The chief directed a number of questions at Warren and K.J. Jeff listened carefully, not knowing what to expect.

"Mr. Abdul wants you arrested immediately. The normal process is to put you in jail until we can prove your innocence."

"In jail!" Mindy said, much louder than she

intended. "He's done nothing wrong!"

"I'm sorry, miss. Your friend had the emerald in his pocket."

"But he's not hiding anything," Mindy cried. "He told everybody he found it."

"I understand," the chief said. "Because of that and a phone call from Mr. Salameh, I'm not going to lock you up immediately. Mr. Salameh offered to take responsibility for you. This is a bit unusual, but I've agreed to release you into his custody, provided you check in with me on a regular basis.

"I'm also giving you until 6 p.m. on Friday to provide positive proof that you're innocent. Otherwise, I'll have to lock you up."

K.J. stared at him in disbelief. "But we leave for home on Saturday," he said.

"I'm sorry," the chief replied strongly. "Your group will have to go without you. *You* aren't going anywhere until this is resolved."

"You're going to make me stay until the necklace is found?" K.J. asked, his brown eyes full of fear.

"Yes. Either find it or prove you didn't take it."

"But...how do I do that?"

"I don't know. Meanwhile, I'll need to take your passport and your visa," he said matter-of-factly, holding out his hand.

Warren reluctantly pulled out a bundle of paperwork and snapped off the rubberband. After shuffling through the stack, he handed K.J.'s documents over to the police chief.

"This guarantees you don't leave the country," the chief replied. "You can go for now, but I want you to check in on Wednesday."

They walked out of the station in stunned silence.

"We've got to find that dumb necklace," Mindy cried.

"I'll bet all this was a set-up," K.J. said. "That witch doctor, Mohammed what's-his-name, doesn't want us on his turf. He wants to control everything."

"Righto," Ali agreed. "He's controlling you right now."

Jeff looked at his watch. It was nearly noon.

"I can't stand this heat anymore," Warren said. "Let's go back to the house. I need to rest a while."

"I can't even think about resting. I don't have a passport anymore!"

Everyone nodded sympathetically.

"Don't worry, K.J. We'll figure something out." Warren wobbled a bit when they reached the Jeep.

"You really don't look very good, Warren," Jeff said. "Not good at all."

"I'll be all right after a nap." Warren smiled wearily.

"I could use an ice-cold soda right about now," K.J. moaned.

"Me, too," Mindy agreed.

"Let's get out of here," Jeff said as they crawled into the Jeep.

Back at Mr. Salameh's house, everyone tried to find shelter from the sweltering heat.

"I'm going to lie down," Warren groaned.

"It's cooler in the house. I'll go hang out with the guys if you want to use my room for a while," Mindy offered.

Warren nodded gratefully and shuffled off in that direction.

"We'll wake you in an hour or so," Jeff said.

In the guys' one-room guest house, Ali stood in the doorway while Jeff, Mindy, and K.J. sprawled on small beds in three corners of the room. Sheets of brightly printed fabric were tied back now, but they could be pulled down to make separate cubicles for privacy. A slight breeze blew through the screened windows. An old unframed mirror stood above a porcelain sink in the corner.

"How hot do you think it is?" Jeff asked, wiping his dripping forehead with a towel.

"I'd say over 100 of your degrees. You get used to it," Ali replied.

"Doesn't it ever rain?" Mindy asked. "I brought my raincoat, but it doesn't look like I'll need it."

"East Africa goes through some serious droughts," Ali answered. "We usually get at least 12 inches of rain in May, our wet season, but we only got a few inches this year."

"We need to pray for rain," Mindy said.

"And soon," Jeff agreed.

"Wait a minute, here," K.J. interrupted. "Can't we talk about more important things? I'm about to be tossed in jail and you guys are jawin' about the weather! What if we don't find the necklace?"

"We'll have to get ourselves a new video man," Mindy joked.

"That's not funny," K.J. said. "How will we convince the police chief that I didn't take the necklace?"

"I've been considering that very problem," Ali said. "Meanwhile, I suggest we keep an eye on Mohammed."

"Yeah. He's the key to all this," K.J. said.

"No. God is the key," Jeff said. "He'll make a way out of this mess."

Suddenly, a loud groan was heard from inside the house.

"What was that?" Mindy cried.

They all rushed through the kitchen and followed the noise to Mindy's room. Warren was curled up on the bed, clutching his stomach.

"What's wrong?" Mindy asked.

"My stomach." Warren's face was tight in agony. "I've never had pain like this."

"What'll we do?" Jeff asked, looking to Ali for answers.

"We'd better get him to the hospital," Ali said. "This could be serious. I'll get the Jeep," he called on his way out the door.

"Please hurry," Warren moaned. "Hurry."

"Can anything else go wrong?" Mindy fought to control her panic.

"God is in control," Jeff said. "Let's stop and pray."

The team huddled around Warren, who was still doubled up in pain. Jeff prayed first, then K.J. Mindy's prayer was mixed with tears and sniffles.

"Lord, we pray that you would help Warren right now," she said. "Please heal his body in Jesus' name."

Everyone agreed and said a quick "Amen."

Jeff and K.J. pulled Warren to his feet and helped him to the Jeep. Ali threw some blankets in the back to make a quick bed. They piled inside and Ali drove off.

"How far is the hospital?" Jeff asked.

"About 20 minutes," Ali replied.

"Let's hurry!" Mindy urged.

Ali screeched into the emergency entrance of the hospital. Warren was getting sicker by the minute. Jeff and K.J. linked their arms and nearly had to carry him through the hospital doors.

Warren's body shook from cold chills. Heavy sweat dripped from his burning forehead, and his eyes were glazed over. He looked like he was going to pass out.

Ali ran to find a doctor, panic on his face. A nurse hurried over, wheeling a gurney for Warren. With the assistance of K.J. and Mindy, he crawled up on it.

Jeff had never felt so helpless. Warren had put him in charge before but had always been close by in case anything came up. He wondered what would happen if Warren couldn't help anymore on this trip. He turned to Mindy and K.J.

"Why don't you guys wait here, while Ali and I go back with Warren?" he said. "We'll talk to the doctor."

They nodded and found two waiting-room chairs.

Jeff caught up with a nurse wheeling Warren into a small examining room. Slowly, Warren looked up.

"I'm sorry, Jeff," he groaned. "I've never been this sick. I'm sure it'll pass."

"It's okay, Warren. You're going to be fine."

After waiting a few minutes, a doctor appeared.

"I'll need some time to examine him," he said matter-of-factly. "You'll have to wait outside."

Jeff and Ali left to join the others.

"How is he?" Mindy said, rushing up to meet them. "Strange things have been happening ever since we got here."

"Do you think the curse the witch doctor put on us is the cause of all this?" K.J. asked.

"Jesus is greater than any curse," Jeff replied. "Let's pray."

The group drew close together, holding hands.

"Jesus," Jeff began, "we know you destroyed Satan, sin, and death on the cross. We commit our lives into your hands. We come in your name for protection. Please break any curse the witch doctor may have put on us. Amen."

"And we pray for our leader, Warren," K.J. added. "Help the doctors diagnose his problem and know how to treat it. Please relieve his pain and heal him from any sickness. Amen."

Jeff looked up. Everyone seemed encouraged. Mindy had a glow on her face again. Ali was watching them closely.

Mindy walked over to Ali. She told him about Jesus and how her life had been changed.

After a few minutes, the doctor came out.

"How's he doing?" Jeff asked.

"Not so good," the doctor replied. "Your friend is lucky to be alive. He has a severe case of malaria."

Chapter 5

The Witch Doctor

Malaria?" Jeff stared in disbelief.

"Is he going to be okay?" Mindy asked.

"Hopefully, he will recover completely," the doctor replied. "We've already started treatment. How long are you planning to stay in Kenya?"

"Until Saturday," Jeff said.

"He'll be lucky if he can go home then." The doctor frowned. "He may need to stay a few more days."

Jeff's stomach churned just at the thought of not having Warren around.

"How did he get malaria so soon?" Mindy wanted to know.

"The mosquitos are extremely bad right now," the doctor said. "Your friend must have been bitten soon after you arrived. Symptoms can take up to a week to develop, but sometimes they appear more quickly."

"But we all took malaria pills," Jeff pointed out. "Why did he get it? Will we get it, too?"

"Those pills are only a precaution," the doctor said. "Your friend happened to get bitten by a mosquito that carried the disease, and there's still a slight chance of you getting it. Using mosquito netting and bug repellant helps, though."

"Can we see him?" K.J. asked the doctor.

"Yes. But only for a few minutes each day. He'll need all the rest he can get."

The doctor showed the group to Warren's room. They walked in quietly. Warren looked like he was asleep.

"Warren," Jeff said softly.

Warren didn't move.

"Warren," Jeff repeated, louder, "can you hear me?"

Warren didn't open his eyes.

"Boy, he's really sick, isn't he?" Mindy twisted her hair nervously.

"Yeah," Jeff said. "I think this is the work of Satan. He's trying to scare and discourage us. I think we're in a battle that we're just not used to—a spiritual battle with sickness and evil powers. We have to keep on fighting."

"We've got to be strong." K.J. flexed a bicep to make his point.

"Is he going to live, Ali?" Mindy asked, tears in her eyes.

"Yes." Ali smiled sympathetically and nodded. "But it will take all his strength away for days."

"I'm gonna check my mosquito net for holes." Mindy blew her nose.

"We need to keep praying," Jeff said, wiping away the tears building in his own eyes. "I still believe this is part of the witch doctor's doing."

"I thought you said Jesus was more powerful," Ali said.

"He is," Jeff replied quickly. "But there's no such thing as too much prayer. Another one won't hurt."

Jeff knew he had confused Ali. He bowed his head and made a mental note to explain later.

"Jesus, we come in your all powerful name again. We ask that you touch Warren by the power of your blood. Please raise him up—"

"And break the curse of this witch doctor," K.J. interrupted, "by the power of Jesus' name. Please show him who is the only true God. Amen."

Everyone agreed.

"Hey!" K.J.'s face broke into a big grin. "Maybe God is preparing us for a bigger battle with the witch doctor."

"Yeah," Jeff said. "Maybe like the story of Elijah in the Bible. God had to show the Baalites who was the bigger God."

"This could get exciting!" K.J. said with enthusiasm.

"Exciting?" Mindy cried. "K.J., would you get real? What are we going to do now that Warren is sick?"

Jeff looked at his sister and then the others.

"To tell you the truth," he finally said, "I'm totally scared to lead without Warren. But I know God brought us here for a purpose. We're not going to be defeated. We'll just have to trust God to be the leader."

Out of the corner of his eye, Jeff spotted Warren trying to lift his head. He was fading in and out of consciousness.

"What's going on?" Warren asked in a whisper.

"You're awake!" Mindy said, her eyes filling with hope. "We've been praying for you. You've got malaria."

"I knew it must be something terrible," Warren replied weakly. "Jeff, you'll have to lead the team until I'm better."

"I'll try." Jeff smiled. He didn't want Warren to know how scared he felt. "The doctor said we could come and see you each day for just a few minutes. You need complete bed rest."

"And plenty of fluids," Ali added.

"Terrific, Capt'n! Bedpans, nurses, the works!" K.J. said with a grin.

Warren tried to smile.

"Check with Mr. Salameh about your schedule," Warren continued, although he had closed his eyes again. "He'll brief you about the tribes you're to visit."

"I'll be happy to assist them with whatever they need," Ali offered. "And I promise to keep them away from elephants and lions this time."

"We'll be praying for you all the time." Jeff put his hand on Warren's shoulder.

Warren was fading out again. "I'll be okay. You guys just complete the work we came to do."

Jeff nodded in agreement, K.J. winked, and Mindy squeezed Warren's hand on the way out.

About four that afternoon they gathered in the living room of Mr. Salameh's house. Jeff and K.J. leaned against the wall. Mindy lounged on a couple of zebra-striped pillows.

"What do we do now, Jeff?" Mindy asked.

"I got our schedule from Mr. Salameh. We don't visit the Masai tribe until tomorrow afternoon, so we can spend the morning working on the video."

"We don't need to work on the video," K.J. argued. "We need to work on this necklace thing."

Jeff scratched his head. His mind was still foggy, but he knew he had to do something to keep K.J. out of jail.

"K.J., how about taking us to the place where you found that stone?" Jeff suggested. "Maybe we'll find some clues about the stolen necklace."

"Good idea," K.J. said. "I'd like to go home with you guys on Saturday. Hate to worry my mother, you know."

"We'd better keep out of the way of that wicked witch doctor, though," Jeff said. "We've got enough trouble."

Jeff, K.J., and Mindy headed toward the village, which bordered Mr. Salameh's house. They walked along the edge of his property and kept out of sight as much as possible. As he watched the people, Jeff's heart filled with love and concern for them. He and Mindy, K.J. and Warren had prayed for the tribespeople and villagers regularly over the previous months.

Women, some with babies tied on their backs with lengths of fabric, were busy preparing dinner. Men squatted in small groups, chatting. Older children gathered wood for the cooking fires that blazed outside their huts. Younger children, running naked and free, squealed in delight as they played games in the red dirt.

"Look at those cute little kids," Mindy said.

"Yeah," Jeff agreed. "They look like they're having fun." He walked a few more steps. "Hey Min, the women are wearing kangas like the witch doctor. Do you know what the writing on them says?"

"Probably brand names in Swahili," K.J. offered.

Mindy shook her head and swatted at his arm.

"I can't figure out how in the world they wrap them so they stay on, but I do know what that writing is," she said proudly.

"Here comes the sermon," K.J. groaned.

Mindy smiled. "It's Swahili all right. But it's proverbs, not advertising."

"You're awesome," Jeff said admiringly.

"Thanks."

They walked on in silence for a few more moments.

"Everyone looks so dusty and dirty," Mindy finally said.

"We're definitely in another world," K.J. observed.

"Let's be careful to keep our distance," Jeff reminded them. "We don't want the village people to alert the witch doctor to what we're doing."

He studied the mud huts that didn't look tall enough for a person to stand up inside. There were different shapes and sizes, but none of them looked like a place he would like to live.

"That's got to be the witch doctor's hut." K.J. pointed toward a very large hut that was more decorative than the others. It was surrounded with people. "Look at how big it is!"

"Don't even think about getting any closer," Jeff said. "Show us where you found the stone."

K.J. led them to an open field leading up a slight hill. "I walked into this clearing to get a long shot of the village," he said. "It was dusk so I was using the light from the camera. It must've hit the emerald because I saw something sparkle on the ground right over there."

Jeff walked to the place where K.J. pointed.

"Let's look around to see if we can find anything," Jeff said.

They parted the grass with their hands and searched carefully for the next few minutes. No necklace. No more loose stones.

"How about up this hill?" K.J. suggested.

"I don't think we should wander too far from home," Mindy said. "There are wild animals out here. Besides...it's getting dark."

Jeff almost laughed at his sister for being such a chicken—until he remembered the game preserve.

"Let's go up just a little further," he said. "I want to see what's over that hill. Besides," he smiled at his best friend, "we've got to solve this necklace thing, or K.J. will never see the girls of Baldwin Heights again."

"And that would be a tragedy!" K.J. added melodramatically.

"Yeah, well, I won't get home if I get eaten by a big lion," Mindy pointed out.

"Relax, Mindy," K.J. said. "We'll protect you."

"Yeah, right."

Jeff led the way, searching the ground carefully.

When he reached the crest of the hill, Jeff was astounded by the vastness of the open bush. The African sky looked like an endless canvas exploding with color—even the hundreds of clouds couldn't hide its beauty.

Suddenly, a strange sound floated in on the wind and froze everyone in their tracks.

"What's could that be?" Jeff whispered as he ducked down.

"I don't know," K.J. said. "But it's coming from over the next hill."

"This is spooky," Mindy said, her voice shaking. "Let's get out of here."

"No, let's check it out, sis. It'll be okay."

Mindy frowned, but she followed the boys as they backed down a few steps and crept around the side of the crest, toward the sound. As they got closer, the sounds became more clear.

"I hear drums. What a great beat!" K.J. exclaimed. "Now all we need is a little bass guitar."

"I think I hear people chanting," Mindy said.

"And some kind of shaking noise," Jeff added.

Peeking over the crest of the hill again, Jeff froze.

"Stay down, you guys," Jeff whispered. "Stay down!"

Jeff couldn't believe his eyes. A long line of people

were slithering like snakes behind a cluster of palm trees.

Mindy and K.J. couldn't help but peek.

"Look," Mindy pointed, "they're shaking some kind of instrument."

"Boy, do I wish I had my camera," K.J. said.

"You guys, those drums are scaring me," Mindy said. "Let's go."

"Wait, wait," Jeff ordered. "This must be some kind of African ritual."

He moved in for a closer look.

"Most of them are women," he said.

"And they don't have much clothing on," Mindy said. "Some are wearing skirts—made of palm branches, I think."

A long line of scantily dressed villagers were following each other through the bush. They frantically beat drums, shook things, and chanted.

Boom. Boom. De Boom. Over and over. Louder and louder. Boom. Boom. De Boom.

"Why would they follow each other into that big tree?" Mindy wondered.

"This is weird," K.J. admitted. "Let's get out of here."

"Look!" Jeff's mouth fell open. "It's the witch doctor! He's the leader of the line."

"I want to go back," Mindy cried.

"Wait!" Jeff yelled over his shoulder. "We can't leave now! Let's see what happens next."

They watched the people do everything the witch doctor did, like children playing follow the leader. Jeff had heard stories of witch doctor's tricks, but he still couldn't believe what he was seeing.

"Look at the power he has over these people," he said in wonder.

"I read that witch doctors can quote one word from the Koran and have people fall down before them," Mindy whispered.

"What's the Koran?" K.J. asked.

"It's the Muslim holy book," Mindy answered.

"That's what makes all this witchcraft so scary. It's mixed with Islam," Jeff said.

"Witch doctors along the coast of Kenya are supposed to be some of the most influential in all of Africa," Mindy added.

Jeff watched as the line formed a circle around a pregnant woman who sat cross-legged on the ground. She was dressed in a black robe and held a small child in her lap. Her grayish-white hair was cut as short as the men's. A look of terror was on her face.

"The little boy looks really sick," Jeff said. "Look at his skinny legs sticking out in front of her. They look like bird's legs."

K.J. and Mindy crouched to follow Jeff as he moved in closer.

"We've got to be still," Jeff whispered to the others, who were trying to stay hidden behind a bush. "We don't want them to see us. We'd have big problems then."

When he glanced back to the gathering, his eyes nearly popped out of his head. The witch doctor was swinging a chicken in the air! The people looked hypnotized. As they sat captivated, the witch doctor started tossing food in the air, then buckets of water!

"I'll bet they're trying to heal that boy," Mindy said. "I read about stuff like that."

Jeff couldn't believe it. The witch doctor began dancing around and pouring the water over the back of the boy's head.

"Can that woman be his mother?" K.J. exclaimed in disgust. "She's shaking the stuffing out of that poor kid. This is making me angry! How can they expect to make him better that way?"

"If they only knew the power of Jesus," Mindy said sadly.

Suddenly, a twig crack behind them. Instinctively, they all ducked into the brush, hoping it would hide them.

Jeff heard heavy footsteps, running straight at them.

The footsteps stopped behind the three of them, and Swahili voices pierced the air. Drummers and dancers were silent and still. A spooky quiet followed.

Jeff was afraid to look up. Finally, he lifted his head and opened one eye in the direction of the witch doctor. Every eye of the eerie gathering stared back at him.

Chapter 6

Green Mamba

Ummmmm, Jeff?" K.J. whispered, poking him in the ribs. "Have you noticed the thugs behind us?"

"I was hoping that if we stayed real still, *they* wouldn't notice *us*," he whispered with a grimace. "I guess we're not as good at camouflage as animals." He inched his head around to look.

Two men built like professional wrestlers stood like stone statues above them. Their t-shirts were torn, as if the fabric just couldn't contain all the muscles.

Jeff gulped.

Like guard dogs waiting for instruction, the two muscle men eyed the witch doctor, who was staring back. His face looked like it might burst into flames.

"Bring them here!" he shouted, throwing a chicken to the ground in disgust.

Jeff stood up and held a hand out to his sister. She moved stiffly, frozen with fear. Somehow, protecting her made Jeff act more bravely than he felt, but he still wished they were all safely back at Mr. Salameh's right now. Huge, rough hands shoved the trembling team toward the witch doctor and his silent mob.

"I'm feelin' sort of puny here. Let's run for it," K.J. whispered. "I'm sure I could outrun them."

"I'm nervous, too, but we'd never get away from these guys." Mustering up all his faith and courage, Jeff pulled back his shoulders and stood as tall as he could. "Besides, we can't back down from this guy. We have to remember that Jesus is greater than any evil power he might have."

As they got closer, Jeff was surprised to see fear on the villagers' faces. But he also saw curiosity in some eyes and anger in others.

The witch doctor waited until the two large men had led Jeff, Mindy, and K.J. into the middle of the crowd, then he began circling them, around and around, like an animal stalking its prey.

The witch doctor stopped directly in front of Jeff, inches from his face.

"Why are you spying on our meeting?" he hissed.

"We weren't spying." Jeff's voice sounded bolder than he felt. "We were just out for a walk when we heard music and saw the dancing." He shrugged. "It looked interesting—more like a party than a meeting."

The witch doctor smirked at K.J.

"You're supposed to be in jail, you little devil."

"I'm no devil," K.J. snapped. "You're the one who's deceiving people. You're the one who's stealing from them. They think you have power, but you're a phony as far as I'm concerned."

Jeff couldn't believe his ears. Mindy stood speechless and trembling.

The witch doctor's eyes glazed over in a dark, evil stare.

"I've put a curse on all of you," he sneered. "You'll be lucky to get out of Kenya alive."

Jeff took one step closer.

"Don't, Jeff," begged Mindy. "Let's get out of here."

"I'm all right, sis. It's time to show everyone who has the most power."

Jeff gently pushed Mindy behind him and stood nose-to-nose with the witch doctor.

"We've come here to bless the Kenyan people," Jeff said calmly. "We didn't steal your necklace, and we don't want to make trouble for you."

"Then why don't you leave?"

Jeff shot a quick prayer skyward, took a deep breath, and plunged in.

"We've come to tell the people of Kenya about the true God," he began. "This little boy will never be healed by throwing chickens in the air or chanting. He'll only be healed by the power of Jesus' name."

Terror and fury filled the witch doctor's face.

"We'd like to pray for this little boy, if we could," Jeff added quietly.

The crowd whispered among themselves.

The witch doctor was raging with anger, but he didn't say a word, so Jeff continued. Turning to the crowd, he began to explain the gospel. In a few quick sentences, he calmly told the people how God had created the world and everything in it, and that he loved them enough to send his son to die for them.

It wasn't until he got to the part about Jesus rising from the dead that anyone moved. At a nod from the witch doctor, the two thugs started toward Jeff but stopped short of grabbing him.

"Let's get out of here," Mindy cried, pulling at Jeff's shirt. "We're in over our heads."

"That's not true," Jeff said. "If God is God, then he can heal this child."

The crowd remained motionless, waiting to see what the witch doctor would do.

Slowly, the pregnant woman, who was still holding the child, stood up. Tears ran down her cheeks.

"My little boy is dying," she said. "I'll do anything to see him healed."

"We can't heal him," Jeff told her honestly. "But we can pray to the God who made your little boy."

The witch doctor jumped up and kicked over the water jug. Then, to everyone's surprise, he stomped off. The muscle men and a few others followed, but most of the crowd stayed where they were, stunned that anyone would stand up to their leader.

Jeff walked over to the little boy and touched his feverish brow. His eyes looked empty and his bones seemed to poke through his skin. His mother sobbed. Behind her, other women cried as well.

He turned back to Mindy and K.J., who both looked paralyzed.

"What are you waiting for?" Jeff wondered. "Let's pray for him."

As Jeff bowed his head, Mindy and K.J. rushed to his side.

"Father," Jeff prayed, "we simply ask that you show yourself to these people. Please heal this little boy in Jesus' name. We thank you that your power is greater than the power of darkness. Thank you, Jesus, that you will do it. Amen."

Jeff looked up to heaven, knowing God had heard his prayer.

The crowd stared at the child. Jeff spent the next few minutes telling the villagers more about Jesus. When he was finished, he smiled at the people and nodded to K.J. and Mindy. They backed away, waving at the crowd. No one made a move to stop them. When they reached the other side of the hill, everyone breathed a sigh of relief.

"I can't believe you did that, Jeff!" K.J. cried.

"Me, neither."

"I'm afraid we'll have to pay for it," Mindy said, her brow creased with worry.

Jeff just smiled.

"I was just as scared as you guys," he said, "but something inside told me I was doing the right thing. It was as if a whole army of angels was standing beside me."

"Do you think the boy was healed?" Mindy asked.

"I don't know. We're just supposed to obey God's Word and pray. It's up to Him to do the healing."

"You did the right thing, buddy!" K.J. said, slapping Jeff on the back. "I'm proud of ya."

"I hope so," Mindy said. "That witch doctor was pretty mad."

K.J. looked in the direction of the witch doctor's hut.

"Don't look now, but I think we're being watched," he said.

Jeff saw the witch doctor out of the corner of his eye. "Looks pretty angry, doesn't he?"

"Let's get out of here," Mindy cried, picking up the pace.

❖❖❖❖❖❖❖

Later that night, Mindy, K.J., and Jeff gathered in Mr. Salameh's living room.

"I don't think I've ever been more scared than the moment those two muscle-bound guys found us in the brush," Jeff said.

"Me, either," Mindy agreed.

"I wish I'd had my camcorder," K.J. said. "It would've been awesome footage!"

"I'm glad you didn't have your camera," Mindy snapped. "Can you imagine what that witch doctor would've done if he knew you had his ceremony on film?"

"Do you think he'll try to get back at us?" K.J. asked.

"I don't know, but I think we should stay on guard just in case," Jeff said, pulling a piece of paper out of his pocket. "Mr. Salameh gave me the schedule he and Warren worked out for us. Tomorrow afternoon we're going to visit the Masai tribe. First, we have dinner with the chief, then we show the *Jesus* movie to the whole tribe."

"What kind of food do you think they'll serve us?" Mindy asked.

K.J. laughed out loud. "How about flaming monkey with breadsticks?" he said.

"Ewww, gross!" Mindy smacked K.J.'s arm. "That's not funny."

"What else did Warren have planned?" K.J. asked.

"Thursday sounds like the most fun." Jeff studied the schedule. "We get to help distribute clothing and food that one of Mr. Salameh's friends sent for the Digo tribe. Wednesday, we'll work on our video. And of course, we have to visit the police chief."

"I'm excited about giving out food and clothes," Mindy said. "I love helping people in need. I only wish that witch doctor would leave us alone."

"Well, like Scripture says, we're not wrestling against flesh and blood, but against the darkness of the land," Jeff pointed out.

The group was quiet for a moment, deep in thought.

"Hey, you guys, it'll be okay," Jeff finally said. "We've got God on our side."

Mindy smiled at her brother, then stifled a yawn.

"I'm tired," she said. "All this excitement is exhausting. I'm going to my room. I'll see you in the morning."

"What's that noise?" K.J. groaned, awakening out of a dead sleep.

"I don't know," Jeff whispered from his bed. "I heard it, too. Something outside."

"Should we wake Ali?"

"Let's see what it is first."

Jeff and K.J. quietly crawled from under their mosquito nets and moved to the window.

"I don't see anything. Do you?" Jeff asked, scanning the darkness.

"No, but I definitely heard something—like someone sneaking around out there."

"Oh no!" Jeff cried as his eyes adjusted to the light. "One of the windows in the main house is wide open—I think it's Mindy's!"

"Let's go!" K.J. yelled as he ran out the door.

"Ali!" Jeff called on his way to the house. "We need your help!"

Jeff and K.J. flew through the kitchen. Ali quickly followed.

"What is it?" Ali asked as he joined them.

"We heard noises outside," Jeff said, out of breath. "Then we noticed Mindy's window was open. She's scared to death of mosquitos. She'd never leave it open."

K.J. was first to arrive at her door.

"Mindy. Mindy. Open up."

No answer.

"Mindy! It's K.J. and Jeff."

The door creaked open. Mindy stood there, rubbing her eyes.

"What's going on?" she asked sleepily. "It's the middle of the night!"

"We saw your window open," Jeff said.

Mindy looked back and gasped. "It was closed before I went to bed. I checked it!"

"See if anything is missing," Jeff said.

Mindy flipped on the lamp and did a quick search.

"My laptop is here. And my glasses...Wait a minute! My jeans were on the dresser. They're missing! And a couple of shirts, too," she said. "I don't believe it! Even my mosquito netting is gone!"

Ali shushed everyone. "Let me explain something," he said. "In Kenya, people sometimes steal things at night. They call themselves 'pole fishers.'"

"What does that mean, 'pole fishers'?" Jeff asked.

"They open your windows and use long bamboo poles with a hook on the end."

"No way," K.J. said, shaking his head.

"Afraid so, chap." Ali smiled. "They insert the pole and hook whatever they can."

"But why would they take my clothes?" Mindy asked.

"To sell them," Ali replied. "American clothes bring good money around here."

"Man, those were my only jeans!" Mindy stomped her foot in frustration.

"You are fortunate you only lost your jeans," Ali said. "Some of the poles have razor blades inside the bamboo so if you try to grab the pole, the blades cut your hand open."

"Are there a lot of pole fishers in Kenya?" Mindy asked.

"No. Only a few. Most people are honest and hard-working, probably like in America."

"I'll bet that witch doctor had them do it!" Mindy said.

"Perhaps." Ali nodded. "I'll check the lock on your window and find more mosquito netting. They won't be back tonight."

"Thanks, Ali." Mindy sighed. "I don't know if I can sleep anymore."

"You'll be okay, Mindy," Jeff said, giving her a quick hug. "Let's all go back to bed."

Jeff squinted when the early morning sun hit his pillow. He groaned, too tired to get up. Thoughts of pole fishers had rattled around in his mind all night. And it was so hot!

He kicked off the sheets and peeked at his watch. It said 6:04. As he turned over to get some more sleep, he saw something move in the far corner of the room. His eyes jerked open.

"K.J.! Wake up!" Jeff yelled.

"What is it?" K.J. moaned.

"I think there's something over by the sink, but it's too dark over there to tell for sure. See anything from your bed?"

"What? More pole fishers?"

"No. Some kind of animal, maybe."

"It's probably outside. Go back to sleep," K.J. mumbled.

"There's something there, I tell ya!" Jeff insisted, leaning over the side of his bed for a better view.

Exasperated, K.J. opened one eye, then they both flew open. He bolted straight up and pointed, terror on his face.

"What?" Jeff said. "What is it?"

K.J. held his hands in the air as if he were telling a fish story—a huge one. He was trying to speak, but all he made was gasping noises.

Jeff looked to the spot where K.J. pointed, then froze.

A three-foot green snake slithered along the floor, stopping behind the old wicker dresser near the door.

"What *is* it?" K.J. asked, his face pale.

"What d'ya mean? What is it? It's a giant green snake!"

"I meant what *kind* is it? Unless..." K.J. paused, thinking for a second.

"Unless what?" Jeff cried.

"Well, Mindy told me about a poisonous green mamba snake," K.J. replied, his eyes wide. "But it couldn't be that kind, could it?"

Chapter 7

The
Sinister Plot

What's a green mamba?" Jeff asked, afraid to hear the answer.

"I hate to tell you," K.J. replied, "but it's one of the world's most poisonous snakes. If it bites you, you'll be dead in 20 minutes."

Jeff scooted back into his corner as far as he could. He could see part of the snake sticking out from behind the dresser.

"Mindy told me about them," K.J. continued. "The black mamba is even bigger. If I remember right, they live in trees and are very likely to attack...especially when they're disturbed."

"Well, I certainly don't plan on disturbing him," Jeff said. "But we're stuck in here—he's between us and the door."

"And I'm pretty sure that Mindy said their bite is deadly enough to kill a three thousand-pound giraffe," K.J. went on, as though he hadn't heard Jeff.

"Enough, already! I wish Mindy wouldn't have told you so much." Jeff rolled his eyes. "She always does her homework, doesn't she? Think she'd have any ideas about why it might climb down from the trees and into our room?"

"Aren't you thinking what I'm thinking?" K.J. asked. "That the witch doctor sent him as our special roommate?"

"Maybe. But we'd have no way to prove it."

"I don't care about proving anything right now," K.J. said. "I just want to get out of here."

Jeff felt his heart thumping wildly. He realized he was trembling. He has been terrified of snakes since a cousin's pet snake had bitten him when he was only six.

"What do we do, K.J.? What do we do?"

K.J. scanned the room.

"We need to kill it," he said. "See a machete or anything?"

"I'm not going to fight that thing!"

"Okay, maybe we should call for help."

"No," Jeff disagreed, "that could make him angry. We need to be as still as possible. Aren't they more likely to attack when they're disturbed?"

They waited. Time ticked in slow motion. Jeff stared at the tail of the snake—and wondered how long it would be before the rest of it came out from behind the dresser.

"Look! He's moving," Jeff called out. "This way!"

"Stay still, Jeff. Stay still!"

Jeff quieted every muscle. His heart was pounding like a giant hammer. He was afraid it might slam right out of his chest.

The green mamba slithered silently across the room, moving closer and closer to Jeff and K.J.

"Let's pray," Jeff whispered in a panic.

"Good idea," K.J. agreed.

"Help, Lord!" Jeff prayed. "Please save us."

The snake kept coming. Jeff looked into the mamba's large, round pupils, and the snake stared back, as if they were in a staring contest. Jeff could see its tongue darting in and out of its mouth. The deadly fangs were much too close.

Oh no, Jeff thought. *He's going to attack!*

Jeff sat frozen. He felt cold fear crawl like a serpent up his spine.

"In Jesus' name," he mumbled under his breath, still staring into the snake's eyes, "in Jesus' name, get away from me."

Immediately, the mamba flinched, lowered his head, and started moving toward the door.

"Your prayer worked," K.J. said in amazement. "I've got an idea."

"It better be good." Jeff couldn't take his eyes off the creature.

"You distract him by throwing something into the corner, and I'll sneak out the window and go get Ali."

"Oh, thanks a lot!" Jeff glared at K.J. "I get to stay with the Jolly-Green-Giraffe-Killer here."

The snake stopped in front of the door, slithering and hissing.

"Okay, okay," Jeff said. "I guess we'd better do something—this guy is getting on my nerves. Go for it."

K.J. quietly grabbed his pants and shoes and prepared to escape. When he was ready, he nodded.

Jeff rolled his pillow into a ball and tossed it as far as he could. It landed beside the snake. Instantly, the green mamba coiled up, darting his tongue rapidly.

K.J. silently eased to the window.

"Do it again, Jeff," he whispered.

"Okay, but he's getting mad."

Jeff tossed his jeans toward the same place. In one swift movement, K.J. opened the window and leapt head first.

Jeff heard a thud, a long "Owwww," and then the sounds of K.J. scrambling away.

Almost before Jeff could realize what was happening, the snake slithered across the room and coiled himself under the window, ready to strike. Jeff wished he was back in California. He'd take fires, floods, *and* earthquakes over snakes any day.

Jeff's t-shirt was wet with sweat and stuck to his back. Time seemed to stand still, and he wondered if this was God's plan for his life—to die of a snakebite on this tiny bed in Africa.

Suddenly, the words "I will never leave you or forsake you" popped into his mind, calming him.

"You're right, God," he whispered. "That's your promise, and I believe it. But I am kind of wondering what's taking K.J. so long."

Noises outside startled him. He looked through the window and saw K.J. and Ali headed his way. Ali had a big ax balanced on his shoulder. Jeff forced himself to be still until they got to the window.

"Where's the snake?" Ali whispered to Jeff.

Jeff pointed toward the coiled serpent.

"Stay put," Ali ordered. "We're going to open the door and hope he makes a run for it. Mambas are shy creatures. He doesn't want to be in there with you any more than you want to be in there with him."

Jeff stared at the door. The knob began to turn. A shaft of light fell across the floor as the door opened. His eyes fixed on the deadly mamba.

The door opened wider, and the snake moved to another corner of the room, as if it knew what was going to happen.

"Where is it now?" K.J. asked from outside.

"In the corner by the sink."

"We have no choice but to come in and kill it," Ali said.

As afraid as Jeff was, he'd been hoping the snake would leave quietly. He didn't want it to die.

Jeff watched as the snake quickly disappeared inch by inch down a hole in the floor.

"It's going under the floor!" he cried.

Ali ran in with the ax poised over his head in striking position. Jeff looked but couldn't see the mamba anymore.

In a split second, Ali swung at the tiny hole in the floor by the sink, splintering it open. He swung again.

The snake came out angry. Coiled and ready to strike, it raised up about two feet in the air.

"Get back, Ali! Get back!" Jeff yelled.

The mamba lurched forward, but Ali's swinging ax pushed him down. Ali jumped back and swung again.

Smash. Smash. Smash. Whack.

Then it was silent.

"Are you okay, Ali?" K.J. asked.

"Yes, now I am," he replied, collapsing against the wall.

Jeff jumped off his bed and ran to Ali. Snake blood was splattered among the splintered wood.

Jeff took a deep breath and sunk against the wall.

"That was a close one," Ali said as he slid to the floor.

"You're telling me." Jeff sighed.

"I think you chaps need to do some more praying," Ali said, his eyes dazed. "It's dangerous to be close to you."

"Jeff, you could have been killed!" Mindy exclaimed when she heard the snake story at breakfast.

"Hey, I'm okay," Jeff comforted his sister. "God was protecting me. I know He was."

"Yeah," K.J. agreed. "Besides, I think it's the snake you should be feeling sorry for. He got the worst of it!" He laughed.

Mindy couldn't help but smile.

By the time they helped pick up the breakfast

dishes, it was beginning to get terribly hot outside.

"What are we going to do this morning?" K.J. asked. "I really want to do some video work."

"Sounds good." Jeff looked over the schedule. "I phoned Warren this morning, but he told me he needs rest today more than a visit from us. So I think we should go into Mombasa and shoot some footage of the city and the coastline. Is that okay with you, Ali?"

Ali nodded. "Just remember not to take pictures of military personnel or police," he said.

"And this time, ask permission before you take pictures of Kenyan people," Mindy added.

"Okay. Okay." K.J. laughed. "I get the picture."

Jeff had looked forward to seeing Mombasa for months. Even though they had arrived at the Mombasa airport, Ali had driven them straight to Mr. Salalmeh's house in Likoni.

It would also be good to get away from the witch doctor and his village for the day, Jeff thought. There might even be a chance to talk with Ali about God.

As soon as they got close to Mombasa, K.J. pulled out his video camera and began taking scenery shots. Jeff was impressed with all the sights and sounds of the bustling city.

Mindy leaned forward and pointed straight ahead.

"Look!" she said. "There, near the entrance to the city. I saw photos of this in a book. They are massive sculptures built out of elephant tusks. They're nearly thirty feet high."

Jeff saw four giant elephant tusks positioned to create two bridge-like openings. Modern buildings could be seen through the arches.

Riding along Mombasa's shoreline, they saw donkeys pulling carts of boxes and baskets. As Jeff and K.J. checked out the ships and large tankers filling the harbor, Mindy informed them that Mombasa was the second largest seaport in East Africa. Boats came and went about a half-mile out.

"I can't believe people are wading in the water," K.J. commented. "It looks awfully polluted and dirty."

Jeff loved watching people along the crowded streets. Men from various tribes were dressed in long-sleeved gowns or suits or shorts and t-shirts. Some wore Islamic caps and turbans.

"How long have you lived here, Ali?" Jeff asked.

"All my life."

"I'll bet you know a lot of people in this city, then."

"I know some, but it has really grown in the last few years."

"How many tribes live in Kenya?" Jeff wanted to know.

"I'll take that one," Mindy interrupted.

"Okay, Mindy." Ali smiled. "How many?"

"Forty-nine."

"Bravo!" Ali said. "Quite the researcher."

"Thanks."

Everyone laughed. Ali laughed the loudest.

"Ali, why is there so much spirit worship?" Jeff asked. "Lots of Kenyans are Christians, aren't they?"

"Spirit worship is practiced all over Africa," Ali replied. "It has always been part of our culture. But since the missionaries came, it is not so prevalent."

"Did the missionaries do a good job?" Mindy asked.

"It all depends on who you talk to."

"What do you mean?" Mindy pressed.

"Since 1850, there has been a flood of missionaries across Africa." Ali sighed. "Along with them came the slave trade...and other things."

"There are always Christians who do good," Jeff said, "and others who don't. They give the real Christians a bad reputation."

"Is that why you call yourselves the 'Reel Kids'?" Ali asked.

"That's right." Jeff nodded. "We want our lives to be real. We truly care about other people—enough to travel around the world to tell them about Jesus."

"I like what I've seen so far," Ali agreed. "As long as you keep away from snakes."

When K.J. laughed, Jeff realized that all they had heard from him since they reached the city was the whir of his camera. They spent the next hour filming. Unlike the villagers, people in Mombasa seemed used to video cameras. As they rode and talked and video-taped, Jeff noticed that Ali was having a really good time. He knew that the friendship they were building would give him a chance someday to invite Ali to experience God's love for himself.

"I need to pick up some things for Mr. Salameh," Ali said, stopping the Jeep at a market near the harbor. "Why don't you wait over there on the sea wall?"

Jeff, Mindy, and K.J. crossed the street and sat where they could watch people walking, wading, and splashing in the dirty water. As usual, K.J.'s camcorder was recording everything. When Jeff saw Ali return to the Jeep, they jumped up and headed back.

Climbing in, Jeff noticed a worried look on Ali's face.

"What's wrong?" he asked.

"I just talked to some friends," Ali replied. "They confirmed something I was afraid of."

"Do we want to know what it is?" K.J. laughed.

"Oh, it's very serious." Ali frowned. "A small group of locals are working with the witch doctor."

"Working on what?" Mindy's eyes grew wide.

"They are plotting together to destroy your mission."

Chapter 8

Forbidden Shoot

Plotting what?" K.J. asked.

"They're working on a sinister plan against you," Ali answered.

"I was hoping you wouldn't say that," K.J. said.

"What can we do?" Jeff asked.

"I'm not sure." Ali shrugged his shoulders.

"Why are they after us?" Mindy asked.

"They know you are Christians, probably because of your association with Mr. Salameh." Ali smiled at Mindy's surprised expression. "News in Kenya sometimes travels at an amazing speed," he added. "The Muslims often disagree with Christians. We believe Mohammed was the only true prophet."

"Do you hate us because of that, Ali?" Mindy asked.

"No." Ali grinned. "Actually I'm learning to like you a lot. Some Muslims, however, are very fanatical. But don't worry. I have an idea. Now, what time do you have to be at the Masai tribe?"

Jeff looked at his watch. He felt like he had been up forever, but it was only 9:30.

"Not until four this afternoon."

"It's a two-hour drive, so we should leave the house around two o'clock," Ali said. "Let's head back to Mr. Salameh's."

"Ali, can you tell us more about Islam?" K.J. asked once they were on the highway.

"When I was studying Islam," Mindy put in, "I learned Muslims believe there is no god but Allah and he only has one prophet, Mohammed."

"That's right," Ali agreed. "And I'll tell you more if you'll explain the personal relationship with God you talked about."

Jeff looked up slightly and thanked God for a great opportunity.

"Don't Muslims pray five times a day and have very strict rules?" he asked.

As Ali was about to answer, they passed a large mosque.

"That mosque is similar to one of your churches," Ali pointed out. "People do a lot of the praying there."

"I heard they try to make it to some place called Mecca once or twice in their lifetime." K.J. commented.

"Yes," Ali said. "It's amazing to me that Mecca is close to where Jesus lived."

"That's right," Mindy said. "A lot happened in that little corner of the world."

Ali rubbed his chin. "What is the most significant difference between Islam and Christianity?" he asked sincerely.

"I'll try to explain it," Jeff said. "Islam is a religion man created, like all the others. It's the story of man trying to reach God."

"What do you mean?" Ali asked. "Aren't you trying to find God?"

"Yes," Jeff answered. "But Islam is an attempt to please God by living according to a difficult set of rules. Christianity is God reaching out for man. Jesus' death meant we'd never have to work for our salvation. We only need to accept it."

"Are you saying that our dedication to prayer is a waste of time?" Ali seemed confused.

"Oh, don't get me wrong," Jeff quickly said. "Prayer is a great thing, but it should be more like a conversation with someone we love. It should come from a *relationship*, not a religion or a set of rules."

"I think I see what you're saying," Ali said.

Jeff hoped he understood because they were just turning into Mr. Salameh's driveway. The four of them piled out of the Jeep and headed into the house.

"I'm anxious to hear about that idea you had, Ali," Jeff said as they walked into the living room.

Ali closed the door. "While I was in town today," he began, "a friend of mine gave me information on some of the witch doctor's other activities. I'm certain you'll find this interesting."

"Interesting, how?" Mindy asked.

"He not only controls the people in the village because they are afraid of his curses," Ali said, "but he is also involved in illegal poaching."

K.J. gave a low whistle. "I assume you're referring to killing endangered species rather than the way my mom fixes my eggs," he said.

"I've heard that poachers kill hundreds of elephants to sell the ivory. They cut off their tusks with machetes or even chainsaws," Mindy gulped.

"That's sick," K.J. said.

"And because of the witch doctor's power, everyone is too frightened to do anything about it," Ali added sadly.

"That includes me," Mindy said.

Ali hesitated a moment, looking unsure. "I found out where they keep the illegal ivory," he finally said.

"I think I know what's coming." K.J.'s face lit up.

"I want to help you fulfill your mission," Ali continued. "Someone has to stand up to this man. Besides, if we just sit back, he'll make it hard on you."

"So what's your idea?" Jeff asked.

"I found out the ivory is delivered to the witch doctor every Tuesday afternoon." Ali paused.

"I still don't get it," Jeff said. "What's that got to do with us?"

"If we could shoot some video footage of him receiving illegal ivory," K.J. caught on to Ali's idea, "we would have an edge on him!"

"And we could turn him in to the police!" Mindy said.

"It isn't that easy." Ali shook his head. "He's got lots of power over the village chief."

"Yeah," K.J. said. "And probably over the police chief, too."

"Maybe," Jeff said. "What time is the ivory delivery?"

"Around 12:30."

"Is it a long ways from here?"

"No. That's the amazing thing," Ali said. "He stores it in a large hut on the other side of the village."

"Well, this is just too easy!" K.J. exclaimed. "That's walking distance from here. Let's do it!"

"We'll have to be careful," Ali cautioned. "We should take the Jeep. Walking through the village with a camcorder would look too suspicious."

"I like the idea. Let's go," K.J. said, reaching for his equipment.

"Wait a minute, K.J." Jeff grabbed his friend's arm. "I'm still in charge. I'd feel better if we checked with Warren."

K.J. looked at his watch.

"There's not enough time to get to the hospital," he said. "Besides, Warren is too sick. This one is your call, buddy."

Jeff didn't like it, but he knew K.J. was right. He looked at Ali, Mindy, and finally K.J.

"Okay," he said at last. "We've got an opportunity to help K.J. out of trouble. I think we should do it."

"Good answer, good answer." K.J. patted Jeff on the back. "It's also a good opportunity to show the people of the village what the witch doctor really is."

"You're right, but we've got to be careful. How can we do this without being seen?" Jeff asked.

"I know the place," Ali said. "I used to play in the area when I was a kid. I've got it all planned."

Within a half-hour, they were in the Jeep again, heading down the dirt road that skirted the village.

"There's an abandoned building near the place where the ivory is delivered," Ali said. "We can film from one of the windows."

"Will we be able to see from there?" Jeff asked.

"I do have a zoom lens, Jeff," K.J. reminded him.

"The deserted building looks directly over the hut where he stores the ivory," Ali replied. "We should have no trouble getting a shot."

"This sounds pretty frightening," Mindy said. She had wanted to stay at Mr. Salameh's. But as the reporter for the group, she knew she couldn't miss a story like this. "Are you sure we can do this without getting caught?"

"I'll prove it to you," Ali said, pulling the Jeep into some tall grass a few hundred feet from the old building. "We'll have to walk behind that cluster of trees. The path comes out right behind the building. I've done it a hundred times."

Everyone cautiously followed Ali behind the trees. Jeff knew Mindy didn't like the whole deal, but K.J. had a look of adventure on his face.

Through the trees, Jeff saw a broken-down brown building.

"No wonder they bring it here," he commented. "This whole area is deserted."

"Exactly." Ali grinned.

Rusty hinges creaked when Ali pushed the door

open. Cobwebs hung from the ceiling, and old wooden crates and packing materials littered the floor.

"I'm trying very hard not to think about rats and scorpions," Mindy admitted in a tiny voice.

Jeff looked at his watch. It was 12:15. The poachers would be there in 15 minutes.

Ali climbed an old rope ladder to a second-story loft. A few beat-up barrels provided cover in case anyone entered the building.

"Come on up," he called. "We can wait here."

After they had all scrambled up the ladder, K.J. positioned himself at one of the windows, wiping the dust off so he could get a clear shot.

"This is great!" he said as he looked through the viewfinder. "I can see the hut and the area surrounding it. I should be able to capture anything that goes on out there."

"Here comes the witch doctor!" Ali called, watching through another second-story window.

"Boy, your friends have good information," K.J. said.

"Now we'll just wait for the ivory to show up," Ali added.

"I don't know why I let you guys drag me into stuff like this." Mindy was crouched down behind a barrel. She didn't want to look out the windows.

"It's safe in here, sis," Jeff said. "Come on, look out the window with me. They'll never see us."

"They might see the camera," Mindy worried as she peeked through the dirty glass.

"Not if K.J. is careful," Ali said. "This building's been abandoned for a long time. No one would think anyone is in here."

Everyone waited. The whine of an aging truck broke the silence.

"Get ready, K.J.," Ali ordered. "The truck will only stay a few minutes."

"I'm ready," K.J. replied. "Rolling film."

A tarp-covered blue pickup truck drove into the area and backed up in front of the hut.

"Thank you, Jesus," K.J. whispered to the sky. "What a perfect angle for the shot!"

"Try to shoot everything they do," Ali told him. "If what my friends said is true, you'll be amazed how many tusks they bring out of that truck."

Two huge men climbed out of the truck.

"Look!" Mindy shuddered. "It's those thugs who grabbed us at the ritual yesterday." She prayed that none of them would look in their direction.

The two muscle men talked to the witch doctor for a few minutes, then began to unload their cargo.

Jeff counted the tusks coming out of the pickup. Just when he thought the truck had to be empty, the men went back for more.

"I don't believe it!" he exclaimed. "I just counted thirty."

"That's fifteen elephants killed because of their greed," Ali said grimly.

"No wonder those guys are so strong," Mindy whispered in disgust. "Elephant tusks weigh up to two hundred and twenty pounds each. From the looks of those guys, I'd say they've been pumping ivory for quite some time."

"Hey," K.J. said, "maybe I should take some tusks home with me!"

"Shhh. I think they're almost finished," Jeff said.

"I hope so." Mindy frowned. "I want to get out of here."

As if on cue, the two men jumped in the truck and drove away.

"Did you get it all on film?" Ali asked.

"Yep," K.J. said proudly. "Closeups of faces and everything."

"Good. Now we'll just wait for the witch doctor to leave and get out of here ourselves," Ali added.

"Just a second...I don't think he's leaving," K.J. cried. "He looks like he's headed over here. What's that box in his hand?"

"We'll be all right if we don't make any noise," Ali said. "He won't find us if he doesn't come up here."

K.J. turned off his camera, and everyone sat very still.

The old door creaked open. Jeff felt a sneeze coming on and quickly put his fingers over his nose.

There were footsteps below. They got closer and closer to the rope ladder.

Mindy grabbed Jeff's arm and hung on. Ali and K.J. turned pale.

Everyone lay quiet.

Anxiously waiting.

Chapter 9

Tropical Theater

No one breathed. Every footstep below brought chills across the back of Jeff's neck. If the witch doctor heard any movement from the loft, they could all end up with K.J. in that prison cell....or worse.

The footsteps stopped somewhere below. Jeff thought he heard a sound, like wood rubbing against wood, but he didn't dare look.

The footsteps began again, this time in the opposite direction. Wide-eyed, everyone looked at each other, frozen in their spots. The steps got closer to the door, then the door shut. No one moved until they were sure the witch doctor was safely away.

"Wow. That was close!" K.J. exclaimed.

"I can't take much more of this tension," Mindy admitted.

"Let's make sure he's gone before we go down," Ali said.

Everyone stared out the window. The witch doctor was making his way to the storage hut.

Suddenly, he turned to look back. All four of them jerked their heads down.

"He saw us! I know he saw us!" Mindy insisted.

In a moment, Jeff peeked again. The witch doctor was heading down the road to the village.

"It's okay," he said with a sigh. "He's gone."

"I wonder what he was doing in here," Ali said with a puzzled look on his face.

"I'll bet we'll find out if we go down and look around." Jeff headed for the ladder.

"Let's get out of here while we have a chance," Mindy recommended.

Jeff looked at his watch. It was almost 1:30.

"We still have some time before we need to leave for the Masai tribe," he said. "Let's take a quick look around here. And then we should stop by the hospital to see Warren for a few minutes."

One by one, they hurried down the ladder and began to search the building.

Ali turned over some old barrels, but they were all empty. Jeff searched under the loft but saw only wooden trunks and boxes. He rubbed the back of his neck and thought a moment, staring at a stack of wooden crates with slated sides. Slowly he realized there was something moving in the crates.

"Ahhhh!" he cried, jumping back. "Do you see what I see?"

"Look at that," K.J. said, automatically aiming his camera. "There must be twenty or thirty snakes in there! Let's hope they can't crawl through those cracks."

"There are different kinds in there," Mindy observed without getting too close. "Black and green mambas, probably cobras and pythons, too. I'll bet they're all poisonous. The witch doctor must have fed them."

"I hope he wasn't getting another one for us tonight," K.J. said.

"I can see why everybody is afraid of him," Jeff added. "He makes his own curses come to pass."

"Let's get out of here," Mindy cried. "One of those little curses might get loose and bite me."

"Good idea!" Ali was the first one out the door.

They rode to the hospital still reeling from the excitement and suspense.

Everyone couldn't wait to tell Warren about their day. The hospital was extremely busy. After checking in with the nurse, they were directed to the doctor's office.

"How's Mr. Russell doing?" Jeff asked.

"Not very well," the doctor answered. "He's resting now, and I think it would be better to let him rest. Why don't you come back tomorrow?"

"Is there anything we can do?" Mindy's concern was evident in her voice.

"Keep sending up those prayers," the doctor said. "He needs help to turn the corner on this attack of malaria."

"We'll be back first thing in the morning, if that's okay," Jeff said, marveling that even the doctor knew they were Christians. News *did* travel fast in Kenya.

"That'll be fine." The doctor smiled. "He should be a little better by then."

"Are you sure you have all the equipment, K.J.?" Jeff asked as they piled into the Jeep.

"Absolutely. Have I ever let you down before?"

Mindy started to say something, but she just shook her head and laughed.

"We won't get into that, K.J.," Jeff said with a grin. He knew Mindy was remembering the time K.J. left the video equipment unattended in the Manila airport and someone had stolen it.

"What do you know about this tribe, Ali?" K.J. asked, changing the subject.

"Mindy?" Ali smiled. "Do you have something to say?"

"No." Mindy laughed. "I don't know a thing about the Masai people."

"What?" Ali asked incredulously. "Do you mean to tell me you didn't study the Masai?"

"Sorry," Mindy apologized. "I didn't know exactly which tribes we'd meet. And I couldn't study everything."

"They are fascinating people," Ali said, pulling onto the road. "Mr. Salameh wanted to come today to introduce you personally, but something came up at the office. He sends his regrets. I think you're going to really learn a lot from your visit anyway. You'll be amazed at the way the Masai live, and you'll love the different types of huts they live in."

"Why's that?" K.J. asked.

"Some of them are four feet high with no windows," Ali continued. "They are made out of cow dung, twigs, sticks, and hay."

"What?" Mindy shuddered.

"You know, ahhh, cow manure," Ali explained. "The women work hours kneading it together. It's a lot of work. Make sure you show respect for their labors."

"Kneading cow manure gets my respect all right," K.J. said with a whistle. "But why are their huts only four feet high?"

"They don't stand up in them. They're only used to sleep in," Ali said.

"Anything else?" Mindy asked.

"It's a real challenge for a Masai youth to become a man," Ali said, turning down a long stretch of highway.

"What do you mean, become a man?" Mindy asked. "I always thought that just sort of happened naturally."

Ali laughed out loud, flashing his gums. "Well, Mindy, the teenage boys must pass a difficult test. Around the age of twelve, they must live for three years in the bush. They can't cut their hair, and they must survive only off the land."

"What do they hunt?" K.J. asked.

"They are required to kill a lion with a spear," Ali answered. "Then they return for a big festival.

That's when they're recognized as a man."

"Maybe we should get K.J. to do that." Mindy laughed.

"Those lions would be frightened of me," K.J. said, puffing up his chest.

"Yeah, right." Mindy giggled. "Anyway Ali, what happens after they become a man?"

"They become village elders. You'll see some of their native dress tonight. Some have their hair covered with mud and their faces painted. You may think it strange, though it is quite beautiful."

"Wow," Jeff said. "Anything else we need to know?"

Ali got a big grin on his face as he drove further into the bush.

"If the women spit at you," he said, "don't be offended. It is a sign of their blessing. That's how they show their affection."

"I hope they don't bless me," Mindy gasped. "I can think of better ways to show affection."

Everyone talked and laughed together. Jeff knew Ali was part of their team now.

Soon the road narrowed and they saw brown huts spreading over the landscape, looking like chocolate chips on top of a golden brown cookie. The huts were large and small, round and square, and several other odd shapes, all set against a perfect blue sky. High in the heavens, streaks of pinks and purples were just beginning to form a beautiful sunset.

As the Jeep entered the village, a procession of villagers walked out to greet them. Several tribesmen followed a tall man with a white beard and strong dark eyes. Rows and rows of multicolored beads decorated the tall man's chest, and a large piece of red cloth was tied around his waist. Jeff was startled by the tall man's perfect smile. His teeth could be featured in commercials for the best dentists and orthodontists in Los Angeles.

"That's the Masai chief coming to greet you," Ali said, opening his door. "He and Mr. Salameh are very good friends, and he set up this visit."

They hopped out to meet him. The chief shifted his spear and extended his hand in greeting.

"Welcome to our home," the chief said.

"We're honored to be here," Jeff replied. "Thank you for inviting our club to your village."

"I have heard about your club." The chief smiled. "Mr. Salameh speaks highly of your work around the world."

"Thank you," Jeff said. "I wish our leader, Warren, could be here, too." He took the next few minutes to introduce the team and explain what had happened to Warren.

"We plan to eat in about an hour," the chief said. "But first I will show you around."

As they walked, the chief told amazing stories about his tribe. Jeff felt privileged to be there.

The chief stopped for a moment. "We are curious about the movie you brought," he said. "Our tribe is not known for listening to new ideas, but I trust Mr. Salameh. He said this is something our tribe needs to know and that you would explain it to us after the film."

Jeff cleared his throat. He looked back at K.J. and Mindy in surprise then nodded quickly to the chief.

"Yes. I'll be glad to say a few words at the end."

"Good." The chief looked pleased. "I believe dinner is ready now."

Strange smells wafted in the air as Jeff, Mindy, and K.J. sat down with the chief at his table. They all looked nervously at each other, everyone thinking the same thing—would they be eating "flaming monkey"?

The chief continued with his incredible stories while wooden bowls of food were set in the center of the group.

"We sent for some Fanta orange soda in case you didn't like what we drink," the chief said.

"What do you drink? I might like to try it," K.J. said.

"It's a very healthy drink. It has made our tribe famous for our perfect teeth."

"What's it made of?" K.J. pressed.

"It's a mixture of cow's blood and milk." The chief smiled. "Very good for you."

"Maybe I'll stick to the Fanta orange," K.J. gasped, finally understanding where the strange smell came from.

The chief laughed. K.J.'s face grew red with embarrassment. The chief laughed some more.

"The Masai are also famous for raising cattle," the chief pointed to a bowl of meat, "so we'll be having beef with ugali tonight. Ugali is corn meal."

Jeff, K.J., and Mindy looked at each other with relief. When the rest of the food arrived, everyone began eating. It took the three of them a few minutes to get used to eating with their hands.

Jeff answered the chief's questions about the

club, then about America. K.J. chewed away happily at the beef, but Mindy was having a hard time adjusting to using her fingers. She was angry at herself for not researching the Masai. She didn't like these kind of surprises.

After the meal was finished, K.J. set up the battery operated movie projector. It was dark now—just right to show the movie. Jeff and Mindy unfolded the large sheet they had brought along to use as a movie screen. The chief sent some of his men to help hang it against the wall of a large hut where everyone could see it.

"We're just about ready," Jeff said to the chief, who was watching everyone work.

The chief called out for some other men to run through the village and tell the people to come.

The chief looked over at Jeff with a big smile on his face.

"The entire village will be here tonight," he said. "I have even asked the children to come."

Jeff wondered if the chief really understood what they were going to show on the screen. Had Mr. Salameh briefed him enough so he wouldn't be offended?

Jeff shot up a "Help!" sort of prayer and knew he wouldn't find out until the movie ended in 30 minutes.

K.J. nodded when he was ready and smiled encouragingly. "Well, at least we won't have to worry about someone turning the lights on in the middle of the movie." He laughed.

"Just make sure it works, buddy." Jeff grinned.

As the crowd gathered, Jeff prayed hard to fight

his nervousness. He felt insecure without Warren around, but he knew God would work in spite of him.

The chief introduced Jeff and Mindy and K.J. Jeff stayed in front with the interpreter while K.J. and Mindy took their place in the back with the projector.

"We're glad to be with you," Jeff began, and the interpreter translated for him. "We want to thank you for your hospitality. This movie we're sharing tonight has been shown in hundreds of languages in places all over the world. It is about a friend of ours who is a very special King. We'd like to introduce you to him through this movie." Jeff motioned to K.J., who flipped the switch.

Jeff didn't know what to expect. Would the people be upset by the message?

It would be a tense half hour.

Chapter 10

Trouble

Jeff moved quietly to sit next to where K.J. was on the ground near the projector. As images and pictures told the story of Jesus on the makeshift screen, Jeff prayed hard for the presence of God to come into the village. He scanned the audience and noticed that everyone was watching with great interest. He didn't understand Swahili, but he knew the movie well enough to know what was being said.

Jeff pushed the light button on his watch. Another five minutes to go.

He waited. His heart beat faster. He was always

nervous when he had to speak in public, but being surrounded by Masai warriors made it worse. He silently reminded himself that God had sent them to Kenya to give the Masai tribe an opportunity to meet Jesus. God would take care of him.

When the movie ended, Jeff stood in front of the dark screen. By the light of a nearby campfire, he dimly saw into the faces of the waiting crowd. Their moist eyes told him the movie had touched their hearts. Some women openly wept; most of the men sat still.

He whispered another prayer and began. "Tonight, this film told you about the greatest King who ever lived."

He waited for his translator to finish those words.

"Jesus is the only person who died and rose from the dead," Jeff continued. "That makes him different from anyone else who ever lived. Jesus offers a simple plan. If we ask him to come into our hearts, he will come inside and become the Lord of our lives."

The translator communicated with emotion, sharing Jeff's words with lots of feeling.

"Tonight I'm going to ask you to pray a prayer," Jeff went on. "If you want Jesus to come in your heart, then say these words after me." He bowed his head. "Lord Jesus, please come into my heart and become my Lord and Savior. Show yourself to me and take over my life."

He waited, wanting to make sure everyone understood.

"Amen."

Jeff looked over the crowd and hoped he was getting through.

"If you meant that prayer, your life will be

changed forever," he added. "We will wait here to talk to any of you who may have questions."

Jeff looked over at K.J. and Mindy, who gave him a "thumbs up" sign. Then he saw Ali. Teeth or no teeth, Ali flashed a brilliant smile.

"Thanks for having us tonight," Jeff concluded, then he moved to join the rest of the team.

He knew the Masai were Muslims, but he hoped at least one or two would come to talk with them. Jeff waited patiently.

At first no one came, then a couple of men made their way to the front. A few women followed. They wore large earrings, multicolored beads around their necks, and the same red-colored kangas as the chief.

Jeff glanced over at the chief and was uncomfortable that he was watching them so closely. At least he was smiling.

For the next hour, Jeff, Mindy, and K.J. answered questions with the small handful of people. The whole time they talked, the chief sat nearby, listening carefully to every answer.

Jeff's stomach began to churn as the last person left and the chief approached. "I hope you liked the movie," Jeff probed.

The chief said nothing, but he was still smiling.

Jeff smiled back, not knowing what to say. "Uh, I think we'll have to leave now," he finally said. "It's getting late."

"I understand." The chief nodded. "I've asked a few young tribesmen to set up a special safari for you tomorrow. We would like to show you a beautiful stream that is a favorite with the local animals. Could you join us for a couple of hours?"

Mindy looked hesitant. "What kind of animals?" she asked.

"You'll be safe." The chief assured. "You'll probably see some hippopotamus, giraffe, and whatever else gets thirsty and comes to the stream."

"We would be delighted to go. Thank you," Jeff said with gratefulness. "What time should we be here?"

"Around two."

Jeff smiled at the chief. "That will be great."

As they bounced down the winding road toward Mr. Salameh's, they all bubbled with excitement. Mindy couldn't stop jabbering about the people she talked to after the movie.

"I hope Warren doesn't mind us going on the safari," Jeff said.

"I'm sure he won't mind." Ali smiled. "He and Mr. Salameh knew about this ahead of time."

"I'm a little worried about what animals we're going to see." Mindy frowned. "I'll never forget those elephants."

"I'm sure it will be fun," Ali reassured her. "The Masai are known for their knowledge of the bush."

"Boy," K.J. said, "what did you think of the response tonight?"

"Amazing, wasn't it?" Jeff declared.

"And I think the chief liked the film," K.J. added. "But I'd feel more comfortable if he'd said something."

Ali had been quiet, and Jeff looked over at him.

"What did you think of the film?" he asked.

"I think I found the answer I've been looking for," Ali replied. "I made my decision tonight to be a follower of Jesus."

Everyone cheered. Jeff smiled toward heaven and welcomed Ali to the family of God.

"I can't wait to tell Warren the great news," Jeff said. "We'll go by to see him before we visit the police chief tomorrow morning."

Suddenly, headlights flashed in the rearview mirror. Jeff noticed that Ali kept checking behind him, a worried look on his face.

"We're nearly home so there is no cause for alarm, but I think we're being followed," Ali finally said.

K.J. almost jumped out of his seat when he turned to look. "Isn't that the blue pickup that dropped off the ivory?" he exclaimed. "It looks like two big guys inside, too."

"Do you think they were watching us tonight?" Mindy asked.

"I hope so," Ali said. "It might do them some good."

As Ali was about to turn onto the dirt road leading to Mr. Salameh's house, the pickup closed the distance between them.

"What are they doing?" Mindy cried.

"They're just trying to scare us," Jeff said, hoping to calm his little sister. "If they can make us afraid, then they can control us."

"They're doing a pretty good job," Mindy admitted.

Jeff kept his eyes on the pickup as Ali drove up

to Mr. Salameh's house. The truck pulled over to the side of the road, and the thugs sat and stared at the four of them.

"I think they're afraid of you guys," Ali said.

"They don't look afraid to me," Jeff said. "What should we do now?"

Ali shrugged "How about getting out of the Jeep and going inside? I hardly think they would try anything outside Mr. Salameh's house."

"And remember to lock your windows and check for long, skinny roommates they may have brought us." K.J. laughed. "I think it's your turn." He nudged Mindy.

"Don't say stuff like that!" The color drained from Mindy's face.

As the four of them got out, the pickup gunned its engine and sped into the night.

Jeff glanced at his watch when he rolled over in his bed early Wednesday morning.

"Hey, K.J., wake up. Time to get going."

"What time is it?" K.J. moaned.

"Around 6:30." Jeff yawned and stretched. "I didn't sleep very well last night. I keep thinking this is a spiritual battle with the witch doctor. We've got to win it in prayer."

"Personally, I'd love to ignore this whole thing and sleep in," K.J. said. "I'm not anxious to face that police chief."

"I know. But I'd have to explain it to your mother if you got tossed in the clink. So get up for my sake, would ya?" Jeff teased, crawling out of bed.

"Thanks for your sympathy, buddy!" K.J. threw his pillow at him. "I just don't know if I'm ready for this. The witch doctor and his goons must really fear Christianity. They're working awfully hard to mess us up."

"I know." Jeff nodded. "It's not going to be easy. Ali said that the police chief is very loyal to the witch doctor. But the scales will be balanced in the end. We've got to be strong and trust the Lord to handle the outcome. Let's pray about it."

The two boys bowed their heads and asked the Lord to show his power by protecting them and seeing that justice was done.

"Thanks," K.J. said with an awkward smile when they were done. "Everything's going to be okay, isn't it?"

"Everything's going to be fine," Jeff replied. "God's in control."

With a renewed sense of peace, they got dressed.

"Let's get the others and get going," Jeff said, tying his shoelaces.

"Race you to the kitchen!" K.J. yelled on the way out the door.

Jeff, Mindy, and K.J. ran for the hospital entrance; Ali followed closely behind. They couldn't wait to see Warren. It seemed like ages since they had seen him last.

Jeff checked in with the head nurse. She smiled as if she were expecting to see him.

"Your friend is doing much better today," the nurse said. "The doctor says it's okay to spend some time with him."

They walked down the hallway and stopped just outside of Warren's room. Peering around the doorway, Jeff said, "Hi, Warren."

A big, familiar smile broke across Warren's pale face. They all crowded around his bed.

"The nurse said you're doing better," Jeff added. "They wouldn't let us see you yesterday."

"I think I've slept the whole time," Warren said. "They've been giving me fluids through these IV's."

"We don't want to make you tired," Jeff said. "But we need to tell you what's been happening."

They took turns catching Warren up on the details of the last few days.

"You're doing a good job, Jeff." Warren winced as he slowly sat up in bed. "Just keep telling the truth and things will work out."

Everyone nodded in agreement.

"One more thing," Warren's tone grew concerned. "I'd be really careful with that video you took of the witch doctor. Use it only if you have to."

"Whatever you say, Capt'n!" K.J. smiled. "I'll hang onto it in case of emergency."

"I'm glad you're with the team." Warren looked at Ali. "It sounds like you're being a real help. Thanks for taking my place."

"It's been my privilege, Mr. Russell," Ali replied. "You have a great club here."

"We wish you could go on the safari with us today," Mindy said, looking at Warren.

"I'm not ready for a safari just yet." Warren took

her hand and gave it a squeeze. "You have a wonderful time. Mr. Salameh tells me the chief is a good man."

After praying again for Warren's healing, everyone said goodbye. Then they headed to the Likoni police station. It didn't take long to get there, and K.J. grew increasingly nervous.

"We're here to see the police chief," Jeff said to the officer at the desk.

A few moments later, the police chief walked out. He had a very serious look on his face.

"Please come into my office," he said. "I've been waiting for you."

As the group sat down, the police chief pulled out the paperwork and slowly scanned it. "I know Mr. Salameh has vouched for you, but we have some new complaints against you. These latest charges are not only against him," he said, nodding to K.J., "but against all of you. I don't care who you know. One more complaint and *I will* put all of you in jail."

Chapter 11

Safari

The color drained from Jeff's face.

"What complaints are those, sir?" he asked calmly.

"The first is disturbing the peace," the police chief replied.

"How's that, sir?" Jeff's brow wrinkled in confusion.

"I am told you broke up a meeting outside the village on Monday," the chief said.

"It wasn't a meeting! It was some weird kind of ritual!" K.J. burst out. Jeff gave him a warning look to be quiet.

"The witch doctor was having a healing service for a child when you broke it up," the police chief continued, as though he hadn't heard K.J.

"We were out for a walk and happened to run into them," Jeff said.

"Don't you understand the power this man has?" The police chief's eyes filled with anger. "It is best you stay out of his way. A witch doctor has the power to take your life, if he wants to."

"Our God is the only one with that kind of power," Jeff said boldly. "He can protect us. Besides, we came here to love the people of Kenya, not to bother the witch doctor."

"I'm also told you bothered the woman with the sick child." The police chief consulted his paperwork again.

"We prayed for her child," Jeff corrected.

"The report says that you tried to confuse her with your beliefs. She is still in great distress over it."

"We only prayed for her, sir," Jeff said quietly.

"I want to know everything you're planning on doing for the rest of your time here."

"We're going on a safari this afternoon with the Masai tribe." Jeff pulled out the schedule to show the chief. "Thursday we are going to the Digo tribe to do some relief work."

"What do you mean 'relief work'?" the chief asked suspiciously.

"We are going to spend some time distributing food and clothing to the poor," Jeff answered.

"Our country is doing fine!" the chief said angrily. "We don't need outside help."

Everyone stood still, all eyes glued on Jeff. He

knew he didn't dare try to argue with the police chief.

"This is your final warning," the chief said slowly, forcefully. "If I hear one more complaint—about *any* of you—I will have you arrested.

"And son," the police chief turned to K.J., "I'm still waiting for evidence that you did not take that necklace. Your time is running out."

K.J. lowered his head and didn't say a word.

The chief held up K.J.'s passport. "I'm not giving this back until you prove your innocence. Without it, you won't be going home," he added.

When K.J. raised his eyes, Jeff could see his fear.

The police chief spotted K.J.'s bag on the floor. "Your camera is in jeopardy, too," he said. "Another complaint and I'm confiscating it."

The police chief surveyed the group seriously.

"Do you understand me?"

"Yes, sir," everyone said together.

"Then go get me some evidence—as soon as possible."

The team shuffled out to the Jeep in silence.

"Things are looking a little grim, aren't they?" Mindy finally said when they were in the car.

"I wouldn't worry too much. As you say, your God," Ali paused and smiled, "*our* God is more powerful than a witch doctor or a police chief. So try to put it out of your mind for now. It's time for a safari."

When the club arrived at the Masai village, they found the chief reading the Bible they had given him. Jeff couldn't believe his eyes.

The chief stood to greet them. "Are you ready to see the stream?" he asked.

"Yes. We're excited," Jeff answered.

"I've been enjoying this book." The chief flashed his perfect smile. "It has some very good stories."

"I hope you enjoy them all," Jeff said.

The chief nodded. "Did you like our dinner last night?" he asked.

"Yes, sir," K.J. said slowly. "I like trying new things."

Jeff saw some young tribesmen getting their spears and other gear. Among them was the translator from the night before. He introduced Jeff, K.J, Mindy, and Ali to the others who would take them on the safari.

Following the barefooted men, they headed out. When they had walked about 15 minutes, K.J. looked around with excitement.

"This is better than the animal reserve we went to the other day," he said.

"I'm still a little nervous," Mindy admitted. "I wish I were sitting in the Jeep right now."

The men laughed. One of the young men turned to Mindy. "We promise to protect you from anything in the bush," he said. "We've had lots of experience here. This is our backyard!"

Mindy smiled in relief.

K.J. pointed straight ahead to some trees.

"Those woods are unusual in Kenya," Mindy spouted her research information. "It's mostly wide-open plains and grasslands."

"Look at all that vegetation," K.J. remarked. "And those rolling hills."

"We're almost to the river," one of the young men said.

Ahead, Jeff saw a beautiful flowing stream that disappeared behind some small hills. The landscape looked like a picture postcard. As they got closer, the stream turned into a river. Jeff was hot from walking in the African sun. He wished he could dive in the inviting water.

"Look! There's a giraffe!" Mindy cried.

Jeff turned to see several giraffes eating leaves off the highest tree branches. One giraffe was competing with a monkey for a spot. A herd of antelope grazed on the next hill.

The hot sun beat down upon them. Jeff knew the animals had retreated to the stream area for shade and a drink of water.

For a while, they all sat on a big rock and enjoyed the incredible sights of the jungle.

Suddenly, the silence and beauty were shattered by the sound of gunshots.

Chapter 12

Poachers

The tribesmen pushed everybody back and told them to wait behind a cluster of trees. The three young men ran off in the direction of the gunfire.

"What is it?" Mindy cried.

"Poachers," Ali said.

"Well, I'm not going to sit here and do nothing!" Jeff felt his pulse race. He took off after the tribesmen.

Ali, Mindy, and K.J. stayed hidden behind the trees.

"What are you going to do?" Jeff asked when he caught up with the young men.

"We're going to try to find out who they are and turn them in to the police," one of them replied.

Jeff stopped to catch his breath. He wasn't surprised to see K.J., Mindy, and Ali appear behind him only moments later. He'd never known K.J. to miss a photo opportunity.

Suddenly, the earth began to vibrate. Being a Californian, Jeff assumed it was an earthquake—until he saw several elephants appear from over the next hill.

They heard more shots, and soon the tribesmen ran off.

Jeff followed the Masai youth as they moved in closer and then hid to watch what was happening. He caught up with them again. Mindy, K.J., and Ali followed a ways behind.

Shots continued to ring out.

"Aren't you risking your life to catch these poachers?" Jeff asked.

"Poaching is illegal. We must try to stop them," one of the young men said. "Our tribe has been looking for these poachers for a while."

Jeff looked back to see where the others were. He waited for Ali, Mindy, and K.J. as the tribesmen went on. After a few minutes, he saw Masai youth coming back from the open field area. Their faces showed defeat.

"They took off when they saw us coming," one of them said. "But we know what kind of vehicle they were driving."

"What kind was it?" Jeff asked.

"They were driving a blue pickup."

"Were there two of them? " Jeff couldn't believe his ears.

"Yes," one young man nodded, "big men, very big. Do you know them?"

"No. But we know who they are. They work with the witch doctor in Likoni."

Jeff looked toward the area where the herd had been. "Did they kill any elephants?" he asked.

"Yes," one boy replied sadly. "They shot four of them. By the time we found them, they had already cut the tusks from two. They usually hunt in the dark, not when the sun is high. They must be in a hurry to fill a big order."

The tribesmen walked reverently back to the scene. Jeff, Mindy, K.J., and Ali followed.

"This feels like a funeral procession," K.J. said.

There was sadness in the young men's eyes as they looked on the bloody scene. Jeff knew the Masai had a great love for their homeland and a respect for those who shared it.

The animals had been shot. There were huge, ragged holes on either side of their trunks where their tusks had been. The elephants' eyes were still open, as if they were unaware of their own death.

"This is awful," Mindy said in disgust.

Jeff walked toward the lifeless and bloodied elephants, anger and pain piercing his heart. The bush had been home to these magnificent animals just a few minutes ago, and man's greed had put an end to them.

"Nature has a way of balancing itself out," one young man commented. "But selfish men put nature out of balance."

K.J. automatically aimed his camera at the scene, but Jeff wondered if the film would be usable. K.J. was visibly shaking.

"Let me know when you have seen enough," one of the tribesmen said. "I'm sorry our safari turned out this way. Later we will send some of our tribe to take care of this."

"As awful as this is," Jeff said, "it was important for us to see."

They walked back to the village in silence. After thanking the chief and the guides, Jeff, Mindy, K.J., and Ali headed back to Likoni.

On the way home, Ali looked over at Jeff.

"What are we going to do about those poachers?" he asked. "The police chief might change his mind if he saw that video."

"I think Warren was right," Jeff replied. "We won't use it unless we have to. Let's stop at the hospital and talk it over with him."

The club huddled around Warren, who was now sitting up in his bed. The doctor was with them.

"You're looking a lot better," Mindy said to Warren.

"I don't think I've seen such a quick recovery." The doctor smiled. "I think one more day in the hospital will do it."

"That's great, Warren!" K.J. exclaimed. "Then you can spend the last couple of days with us."

"Hold on." The doctor held up his hand. "He's still pretty weak, but I think he can make the flight home." He looked at Warren. "I'll be by again in the morning." He turned and left.

With the doctor out of the room, Jeff brought up

what he and Ali had discussed.

"Warren, on the safari today we ran into some poachers," he said. "And we think they're the same ones we have on the videotape. The Masai tribesmen saw their blue pickup. Do you think we should take it to the police yet?"

"Well," Warren responded slowly, "that additional bit of information certainly makes the tape more valuable. But I'd still hold on to it. The witch doctor has a lot of power, and a videotape from foreigners would probably be regarded with some suspicion. Let's use it only if we have to."

"That's what I thought you'd say." Jeff smiled.

With that, the team prayed for Warren and said goodnight.

When Ali pulled the Jeep into the dirt driveway of Mr. Salameh's twenty minutes later, Jeff's heart skipped a beat.

"Look!" he pointed. "It's the blue pickup!"

Chapter 13

The Mission

Jeff, K.J., Mindy, and Ali looked at each other in shock.

"What are they doing here?" Mindy wondered aloud. "In *our* driveway?"

"I don't know, but we need to call the police," Jeff said.

"Maybe we should run for it. I certainly don't want to face them!" K.J. exclaimed.

Ali motioned for everybody to calm down. "I don't think they're going to do anything now," he said. "Let's see what they want."

"Ali's probably right," Jeff agreed. "We need to face them."

Everybody followed Ali toward the blue pickup. The thugs were sitting in the cab with smirks on their faces.

"What do you want?" Ali asked.

"The witch doctor wants to see you," the man behind the steering wheel said. "He wants to make peace with you."

"I am certain you'll understand if we are skeptical." Ali eyed the man suspiciously.

"You'll have to come and find out," the man replied. "He'll meet you at the edge of the village at eight o'clock in the morning."

"We're not going to make any deals with him." Ali had locked his gaze on the man.

"He'll be waiting in the area where you said you found the stone." The man started the engine and drove away.

"What do you think the witch doctor is up to?" Jeff asked.

"There's only one way to find out," Ali said. "We'll meet him in the morning."

"I guess there's no harm in talking to him." Jeff nodded. "Maybe he's had a change of heart."

"I think he's setting a trap for us." Mindy pulled nervously on her ponytail.

"We can't be afraid of him, Mindy," K.J. pointed out.

"We'll find out what he's got on his mind in the morning," Jeff said. "Let's get some sleep. Sounds like we have an exciting day tomorrow."

"When's he going to get here?" K.J. asked impatiently, kicking at the ground with his feet. "We're where we said we would be. This is where I found his emerald."

"It's not quite eight," Jeff pointed out. "I'm sure he's on his way."

Mindy pointed down the road. "There he is."

The witch doctor was leading a procession of people.

The thugs flanked him like trained Dobermans. Not far behind was a crowd of villagers. Jeff searched the crowd for the woman whose little boy they had prayed for, but he didn't see her.

"Good morning," the witch doctor said as he stepped in front of Jeff.

"Good morning," Jeff replied evenly. He could almost see some evil plot in the witch doctor's eyes. "Your friends said you wanted to talk to us."

"That's right. I want to make you an offer."

Jeff took a deep breath. Ali stood close by his side.

The crowd listened carefully. The witch doctor moved in closer. "Our people don't need your message about Jesus," he said. "I'll make a deal with you. I won't press charges against your friend if you promise not to visit any of the tribes anymore. That includes not showing your movie or saying anything else about Christianity."

The crowd nodded.

Jeff looked at Ali and saw the anger rising on his face. His own heart was beating so fast he was afraid it would burst. He turned back to the witch doctor.

"I'm sorry," Jeff said, trying to stay calm. "God sent us here with a purpose, and we intend to complete our mission. We will not bargain with you."

A dark scowl came over the witch doctor's face.

"Then if you think your God is so great," he sneered, "you won't be afraid to put him to the test."

"What kind of a test?" Jeff asked.

"It hasn't rained for months," the witch doctor declared. "If your God is so powerful, then he can make it rain."

"We believe he could," Jeff said. "But what are you getting at?"

The witch doctor smirked. "I will gather the people of the village tomorrow afternoon," he said. "We will give you an opportunity to make it rain. If it doesn't, then we'll all know your God is powerless."

The crowd applauded. Jeff felt the pressure building.

"Why haven't you been able to make it rain?" he asked. "Witch doctors have the power to do that, don't they?"

"My powers are not in question," the witch doctor quickly replied. "We want to see if your God is as great as you say."

Jeff felt the eyes of the crowd on him, piercing like daggers. He looked down to the ground for a moment, praying for wisdom.

"If your God is so great," the witch doctor hissed, "you will meet me in the middle of the village at one tomorrow."

Jeff looked at Ali. He wished Warren were here.

The witch doctor was getting impatient.

"What's your answer?" he demanded.

The crowd was silent, waiting expectantly.

"We'll take the challenge," Jeff finally said, slowly and calmly. "Our God is able to bring rain at any time. You will know who the real God is. And so will your people."

The crowd erupted in cheers and loud cries. The witch doctor only smiled.

Mindy rushed up to Jeff. "Are you crazy?" she cried. "Don't you know you're walking right into his trap?"

Jeff looked at his friends. "God sent us here to prove his power," he said. "It's our reputation that might get hurt, not His. God will be God."

The witch doctor grinned as if he had already won. "Then you will meet me tomorrow?" he asked.

"Yes," Jeff said. "We'll be here."

The witch doctor laughed as he and the crowd walked away.

"Why did you do that, Jeff?" K.J. asked.

"Do we believe God is greater?" Jeff responded. Everyone nodded.

"Then we've got to relax," Jeff said. "It will be just like the story of Elijah and the Baalites."

"The witch doctor is up to no good," Ali warned.

"God is greater than any witch doctor's dirty trick," Jeff said. "Come on. Right now we've got to get ready to go to the Digo tribe. We've got a mission to do."

"Let's go find Mr. Salameh," he said as he and the rest of the group walked back to the house. "He'll tell us what to expect today."

Ali nodded. "I'll take you to his office. The truck with the relief supplies is loaded and waiting there.

Then it will be an hour drive."

When Ali pulled the Jeep in front of the Mombasa Tea Company office, Mr. Salameh waved out his window, then walked out to meet them.

"It's good to see you," he said, extending his hand to Jeff. "I'm sorry I haven't been home to spend more time with you this week. I hope Ali is taking good care of you. I've had some unexpected things happen."

"We've had unexpected things happen, too," Jeff said.

"I've heard about them." Mr. Salameh chuckled. "Anyway, the truck is loaded. Ali knows where to go. It's a bumpy trip, but I know you'll like these people. I've been to their village a few times."

"Oh, I know we'll have a great time," Mindy commented. She was excited. She loved helping people in practical ways—almost as much as she loved to watch ministries develop as a result of churches watching their videos. That was one purpose of the Reel Kids club—to touch the poor of the world.

Mr. Salameh walked to the back of the truck. The door was open and stacked nearly to the top with boxes. "My prayers are with you," he said. "Most of the clothes in here are brand new. We also have bolts of material so clothing can be made. And there is a month's worth of rice, cornmeal, and powdered milk for the children."

"Thanks so much, Mr. Salameh," Jeff said. "We'll let you know what happens."

Ali shut the back door, and everybody jumped in, anxious to get going on their hour-long journey. It would be another chance to see the beautiful African plains.

Jeff could tell by the heat that it was just past noon when they pulled into the Digo village. As they got close to the first row of huts, a number of little, naked children ran out to greet them, surrounding the truck. The men followed.

The Digo were dressed different than the Masai. Some wore white robes while others had shorts and ragged t-shirts. The women wore kangas. The huts were made of whitewashed coral blocks.

"Oh no," K.J. groaned. "Those buildings remind me of the police station at Likoni."

Ali drove slowly. Kids hung on the sides of the truck as it crawled along the dirt road.

"Look at those cute kids," Mindy cried as she waved. "I hope we've got some good things for them."

"Mr. Salameh didn't tell you," Ali smiled, driving carefully through the crowd, "but we've got toys for them in the back, too." Ali drove to the center of the village. "These people are very fun to be around," he said. "They are extremely poor, yet live a very happy, simple life."

"Are many of them Christians?" Mindy asked.

"Not many." Ali shook his head. "Most are Muslims. I know Mr. Salameh keeps telling them about Jesus. Perhaps I'll come along to help him next time."

As the team climbed out of the truck, they were mobbed by hundreds of people. The crowd parted as the chief walked up. He greeted each member of the team with a smile, giving K.J. special permission to film his people.

"We're very glad you are here," the chief said. "We've got some things planned for you this afternoon. And we would like you to stay and eat with us."

K.J.'s face turned a little pale, but he kept quiet. He didn't want to offend anyone.

"How kind of you," Jeff answered for them. "We would be honored to join you for dinner. We would like to give out the gifts now. Is this the best place?"

"Yes." The chief nodded. "I have told my people to line up. That is the way we've done it in the past."

"Okay. Let's get busy."

For the next two hours, they handed out the clothes, toys, and sewing material. Each gift was received with a look of joy on the people's faces.

"This is what life's all about," Jeff commented happily, "giving to others."

"Yeah. It sure beats the rat race at home," Mindy said as she handed a toy to a squealing toddler. The child's eyes lit up in delight. Mindy smiled.

"I wish I could bring every Christian kid on one of these trips," Jeff said. "It would change their hearts forever."

When Jeff's box was empty, he helped Ali, who was still distributing children's clothing. The return address on the box had said, "The Bubblegum Closet, Gig Harbor, WA, USA." Jeff looked around and noticed that things had been sent from all over the world. He shook his head in awe of the Lord's power and planning.

"Except for the food, that's the last box," Ali said as he handed out the final piece of clothing.

"And I think everybody got something," Jeff added.

"Where do we take the food?" Mindy asked.

"The chief said he'd send some of his men to store it," Ali answered.

"This has been so much fun!" Mindy sighed contentedly. "Isn't it wonderful that giving to others brings us so much pleasure?"

They spent the rest of the afternoon walking around the village.

"Look at those musical instruments," Mindy said, pointing to some drums and shakers.

"I'll bet this tribe has a good time," K.J. added.

"Speaking of a good time," Jeff put in, grinning slyly, "maybe we'll get some of that 'flaming monkey' tonight."

"I knew you'd say that," K.J. moaned, putting his camera down for the first time since they'd arrived in the village.

At dinner, Mindy, K.J., Jeff, and Ali were seated in a place of honor next to the chief. Chicken, ugali, rice, and coconut were served. Then came a special vegetable called *skum a waki*.

After dinner, the villagers played drums and danced for their visitors.

"That was wonderful!" Mindy exclaimed, her eyes shining. "I wish we could stay longer."

"Me, too," Jeff agreed. "But we should probably head back."

"Yeah," K.J. said glumly, "we've got a big day ahead of us tomorrow."

Chapter 14

The Village Showdown

Jeff felt the warm, bright rays of light coming into the room, reminding him that it was Friday—showdown day. He still wasn't sure why he had accepted the witch doctor's challenge, but he knew that showing the character of God was what the Reel Kids club was all about.

"Lord," he mumbled as he stayed in bed a few more moments, "I've seen you in action many times before. I know I can trust you. But I still feel a little frightened." He paused, waiting for his heart to slow down. "I've really gone out on a limb for you this time, God. You're in control."

He rolled over and saw that K.J. was watching him.

"I hope Warren can come with us," was all K.J. said.

"Me, too," Jeff sighed.

"Is Mr. Russell ready to be released?" Jeff asked the head nurse. Mindy, K.J., and Ali stood behind him.

"I believe so," she replied. "Why don't you go to his room? The doctor is with him."

When Jeff walked into Warren's room, he couldn't believe his eyes. Warren was fully dressed and sitting on the edge of the bed.

"Hi, guys," Warren said with a grin.

"Boy, Capt'n! You look like you've been raised from the dead," K.J. exclaimed.

"I really feel like I have." Warren nodded his head.

"You're looking at a miracle," the doctor said. "Mr. Russell should have been here much longer than this. I've checked him over, and he is almost completely well."

"That's wonderful!" Mindy bounced up and down excitedly.

"Your prayers worked," the doctor said. "I hope you have the best of luck on the rest of your trip."

"Yeah," K.J. replied. "We're going to need it."

A big smile crossed the doctor's face. Jeff wondered if he'd heard about the showdown through

Kenya's remarkably fast "news system."

"Take care of him," the doctor added. "He'll be fine if he gets some rest in the next couple of days."

"We'll take *really* good care of him," Mindy assured the doctor.

On the drive back to Mr. Salameh's, Jeff filled Warren in on the latest events.

"I think we should have a good prayer meeting," Warren said. "We don't want to go out against the witch doctor in our own strength. We'd be in trouble for sure."

"What if it doesn't rain?" K.J. asked.

"Well," Warren said, "we'll look like fools. But I'd rather be a fool for Jesus than for anybody else."

After arriving home, they gathered in the living room for a time of prayer. Joining hands and hearts, they called on God to show his power.

"Jesus," Jeff had never felt so weak in his life, "we ask you to prove yourself to the village today. Expose the powers of darkness, and show the people your love. Show them you are the only God."

One by one, Warren, K.J., Mindy, and even Ali prayed. When they were finished, they looked at each other in awe. They knew God was with them.

"A Scripture verse came to my mind while we were praying," Mindy said. "It's Jeremiah 32:27: 'Is there anything too hard for me?'"

"That's an amazing verse," Warren agreed. "I think God is trying to encourage us to trust Him today."

❖❖❖❖❖❖❖

Around 12:30, they started toward the village. As they got closer, they could see how much the word had spread. Hundreds of people had gathered for the big showdown.

"Look! There's the witch doctor!" Mindy cried. "I was sort of hoping he wouldn't show up."

"What's he doing?" K.J. asked.

"It looks like some kind of ritual," Warren said.

"He's probably trying to put another curse on us," K.J. said with disgust.

The witch doctor was holding a large pitcher of water. A group of women chanted loudly next to him. The noises sounded like they were from another world.

As Jeff moved closer, he felt a dark presence gripping everyone there. He knew it was time for spiritual warfare.

The witch doctor stopped when he noticed the arrival of the group.

"I didn't think you would show up," he sneered. "You don't really think you can make it rain, do you?"

"No. We can't make it rain." Jeff smiled on the outside even though he was frightened inside. "But the one who made the clouds and the sky is here with us. His name is Jesus."

At the mention of Jesus' name, the witch doctor's face quivered, then he began to laugh.

"You'll be the joke of the village in a while," he scoffed. "You shouldn't have taken my challenge."

Jeff spotted the thugs sitting nearby, smirks on their faces.

The crowd grew bigger and bigger. Jeff and the team nervously waited...and prayed.

At one, the witch doctor climbed up on a large rock in front of the crowd.

"These Christians are from America," he announced loudly. "They think their god is greater than Allah."

The crowd booed.

"They've got till three o'clock to make it rain," the witch doctor continued in a loud voice. "We'll see how great their God is."

Warren whispered something to Jeff.

"That's a good idea, Warren," Jeff whispered back. "Let's see if they'll agree to it."

Standing tall, Warren walked to the rock and climbed up. He looked more like a mountain climber than a man who was just released from the hospital.

"We're here because we want you to know who the real God is," Warren began. "We know you need rain for your crops, and we want to pray to the maker of heaven and earth to bring it."

The crowd began laughing and yelling things. Warren paused until the people quieted down.

"Why don't we make this a fair challenge?" he asked.

The superior smirk disappeared from the witch doctor's face. People whispered. Again, Warren waited for the crowd to be quiet. Then he cupped his hands around his mouth so he could be heard better.

"We'd like the witch doctor to show his power," Warren said. "We'll let him go first. We'll give him until three o'clock, and if it doesn't rain, then we'll pray. You can give us until dark."

The crowd applauded. Jeff was amazed that they liked the idea. The witch doctor clenched his fists in anger, but he had no choice now. He moved to the front of the crowd and called some women over. Then he began to go through his rituals.

The witch doctor chanted and danced for some time. Then he looked like he was trying to hypnotize some chickens. After swinging the birds in the air, he took pitchers of water and threw them into the air as well.

"Obviously," K.J. whispered, "this is a multi-purpose chant used for healing children *and* bringing rain."

Nothing happened.

Everyone waited, occasionally looking skyward. The crowd began to grow impatient. Soon they were mocking the witch doctor.

Jeff looked at his watch. It was three o'clock.

The witch doctor turned to him and hissed, "It's your turn now."

Jeff walked to the rock. Warren, Mindy, and K.J. followed close behind. Ali stayed on the edge of the crowd, praying. Standing in a small circle, Jeff led them in a couple of worship songs.

The witch doctor began to scream loudly. Jeff ignored him and continued singing. Then joining hands with the rest of the team, he looked up to heaven.

"Lord," Jeff prayed, "we ask you to bring rain to this land. Have mercy on these people, and show us your power. Amen."

"Amen," Warren echoed.

They sat down. Jeff looked for Ali, but he had disappeared. He checked his watch. He knew it would be dark soon.

The witch doctor's followers laughed and mocked them. The crowd grew impatient. They began yelling and stomping their feet.

Jeff looked up to the sky. He noticed a couple of clouds, but they looked pretty dry.

Then a man picked up a piece of fruit. Jeff ducked as he saw it flying toward him. The crowd got more and more rowdy and began laughing louder. Suddenly, they were throwing a shower of things at Jeff and the others. Mindy ducked as she tried to dodge the flying objects.

The crowd was turning into an angry mob. They moved in closer and began to surround Jeff, Mindy, K.J, and Warren.

"You're a bunch of phonies!" the witch doctor shrieked.

"Look at them!" another yelled. "Their God doesn't exist!"

"Somebody do something!" Mindy cried. "Before they kill us!"

Chapter 15

Prisoners

Jeff knew they'd fallen right into the witch doctor's trap. The mob would do the witch doctor's dirty work for him.

Panicked, Jeff looked around for a way out. Over the heads of the crowd he saw the police chief and a few of his men running in their direction. For a second he wondered whether they would be arrested or rescued.

Then strangely, he felt peace. Relief came over his whole being. He grabbed Mindy's hand.

"It's the police chief!" he yelled to the others. "Come on!"

Jeff, Mindy, K.J., and Warren moved through the mob toward the police chief. The policemen made a human wall around the team, protecting them like uniformed angels.

Upon the arrival of the officers, the crowd quickly calmed and started to disperse, the villagers heading back to their huts.

Jeff was glad to be alive. He gave Mindy a quick hug.

The police chief turned to them. He was clearly angry. "Why must you always disturb the peace?" he yelled. "This is the last time. You are all under arrest."

"What?" Jeff couldn't believe what he was hearing.

Warren put a calming hand on Jeff's arm. "I'm looking forward to lying down right now," he said weakly, "even if the bed is in jail. But don't be discouraged, Jeff. God's timing is always different than ours."

"Timing," Jeff said glumly. "It's dark. There's no rain. We're the fools now."

"Yeah." K.J. nodded. "The only thing left for us is an African prison cell." He nervously fidgeted with his camera bag.

"I knew you shouldn't have taken the witch doctor's challenge." Mindy was angry and scared. "He planned this all along."

"He didn't care about the rain," K.J. said. "He set us up for all this."

The chief of police hurried the team into his Land Rover. After getting them inside, he went to help his officers send home the few villagers who had stayed to see what would happen.

"This is my last trip, Jeff," Mindy said. "From now on I'm staying in our safe little neighborhood."

"I really wanted this trip to Africa to be our best." Jeff couldn't hide the disappointment he felt. "Why has God let us down?"

Warren turned to him. "It isn't over yet, Jeff," he said.

"Yes, it is," Jeff argued. "K.J. is in big trouble because of the necklace. We never did find any proof that he didn't do it. And who knows what they'll do to us."

Out the window of the police vehicle, Jeff spotted the witch doctor and his t-shirted "guard dogs." They were waving and laughing out loud. He looked away in disgust, knowing he couldn't take anymore.

"Do you think Mr. Salameh can help us?" Mindy asked.

"I'm not sure," Warren answered. "He's a well-respected man, but he's also a Christian."

"Hey, Capt'n. Think that 'prisoners always get one phone call' rule is international?" K.J. cracked, trying to lighten the mood.

"I don't know."

Jeff saw the police chief walking toward them.

"No matter what, you guys, let's be thankful," Warren added quietly. "The police may have saved our lives."

The police chief climbed into the driver's seat. He looked back, shaking his head. "I warned you," he said. "Why don't you Americans ever listen?"

"Sir, this whole thing was not our idea."

He waved his hand to silence Jeff.

"I don't want to hear any excuses. I'm taking you straight to jail," he said, starting the vehicle.

The words felt like knives through Jeff's heart.

As the Land Rover stopped in front of the station, the chief got out and opened the door. "All right. Everyone inside," he ordered.

Heads down, the team shuffled inside. The police chief stopped them near his desk.

"Please put all your belongings into this box," he said.

The police chief went into his office, leaving a guard to watch them.

As K.J. went through his camera bag, he pulled out the tape of the poachers. "Hey, you guys," he whispered. "I forgot about this."

Mindy's face lit up. "Maybe now would be a good time to use it," Jeff said.

"What good will it do?" K.J. asked. "The witch doctor has probably paid off the police."

A big grin came over Warren's face. He took the video and walked back to the police chief's office.

After a few minutes, Warren and the chief returned.

"He confiscated the tape," Warren said with a shrug.

The team was led into the prison quarters and placed in a cell. The prison door shut with a metal clunk. They all hung their heads in silence.

Jeff couldn't believe this had happened to them. He wondered if he would see his parents and his home again.

Chapter 16

The Thief

Warren rested one of the bunks in the small cell while Jeff, K.J., and Mindy sat in silence on the other, lost in disappointment and fear.

"Hey, did you hear that?" K.J. asked suddenly.

"Hear what?" Mindy muttered. "I think you're imagining things."

"No, K.J. is right," Jeff said. "It's a rumbling noise, and it's getting louder!"

The sound rolled across the sky.

"It's thunder!" K.J. exclaimed. "It's thunder!"

"I hope there's water mixed with it." Jeff's eyes grew wide.

The sound of rain hit suddenly, like nails pounding on the tin roof. They all looked up, as if they could see through the ceiling.

"People would think you've never seen God answer prayer before!" Warren said from his bunk, grinning widely.

Water began dripping through the holes in the ceiling. Jeff jumped up and started dancing, leading the others in celebration.

"Quiet in there," the guard called.

"It's raining!" Jeff cried.

"I don't care what it's doing outside. Be quiet in there!" the guard ordered.

Jeff heard loud voices from the front office. "It sounds like people cheering," he said.

The police chief rushed in, looking a little flustered. "It seems your God answered your prayers," he said simply.

"He sure has!" Mindy cried.

The police chief fumbled with the key then opened the cell door. "Our department has been working with the Masai chief for some time on an illegal poaching case," he explained. "He just told me about the incident that happened while you were visiting them. The Masai have identified the poacher's pickup as the one belonging to the witch doctor's men."

Jeff listened in amazement.

"I watched the video Mr. Russell gave us," the police chief continued. "We now have enough proof to put the witch doctor and his friends in prison for illegal poaching. I just sent my men to pick them up."

Mindy's mouth fell open.

The police chief pointed toward the front door, where a noisy crowd was dancing in the downpour.

"The villagers want you to come out," he said. "They believe in your God because it hasn't rained for months. They know it wasn't the witch doctor because he has tried many times before."

Jeff, Mindy, K.J., and Warren walked outside. The crowd cheered loudly.

Jeff saw the Masai chief and his tribesmen, all grinning from ear to ear. They explained that Mr. Salameh had brought them to talk to the police chief about the poachers.

Next to the Masai chief was the pregnant woman whose little boy they had prayed for. He looked completely wet—and completely well.

Ali and Mr. Salameh stood cheering with the rest.

"One more thing you need to know," the police chief said, putting a hand on K.J.'s shoulder.

"What's that?" K.J. asked.

"We solved the mystery of the stolen necklace."

They all moved in closer. Everyone wanted to hear about this.

"A very strange thing has happened." The police chief pulled out a sparkling green necklace from a plastic bag. The stones matched the emerald K.J. had found. "One of my men found the necklace—with one stone missing—hanging high in a tree near the place where you found the stone. It took him two hours to get it away from the baboons. Apparently, they were the ones who took it from the witch doctor's hut."

Everyone laughed.

Through the rain, Jeff watched the villagers dance in celebration. Ali grinned his toothless grin as he walked up to him.

"Your God—my God—is far greater than any others." Ali gave him a big hug.

Jeff looked at him with tears filling his eyes.

"Ali," he said, "I'll never forget Africa after all this. And I promise I won't forget you."

"Neither will I," Mindy cried.

K.J. stared at the mysterious necklace the police chief held in his hand and shook his head. "Neither will I!"

OTHER RESOURCES

Tracking Your Walk
This journal will help you record your prayers and thoughts and encourages you to pray for people around the world. Includes maps and country information.
ISBN: 0-927545-70-5
$12.99

Walking With God
A sequel to the best-selling *Tracking Your Walk*, this new journal guides young people in developing a strong prayer life, spending time with God, experiencing God's faithfulness, and learning how they can make a difference in God's world.
ISBN: 0-927545-79-9
$12.99

GO Manual
This informative manual lists Youth With A Mission's outreach opportunities around the world.
ISBN: 0-927545-77-2
$5.99

To order, contact: YWAM Publishing
PO Box 55787, Seattle, WA 98155
1-800-922-2143
www.ywampublishing.com

For information to help you go on your own adventure:

King's Kids International Service Team
Email: info@kkint.net

Collect all of the

Reel Kids Adventures

by Dave Gustaveson

The Missing Video
An exciting adventure into Communist Cuba. Will a missing video send the Reel Kids into an international nightmare?
ISBN: 0-927545-60-8
$6.99

Mystery at Smokey Mountain
A spine-tingling mystery awaits Jeff and the media club in the Philippines as they attempt to help the poor at Smokey Mountain in Manila.
ISBN: 0-927545-65-9
$6.99

The Stolen Necklace
In Kenya, the Reel Kids find a jewel that causes problems bigger than the wild animals of the African jungle.
ISBN: 0-927545-71-3
$6.99

The Mysterious Case
Jeff couldn't imagine how much one small mistake would cost them. A mysterious suitcase leads the Reel Kids on a collision course with the deadly Colombian drug cartel.
ISBN: 0-927545-78-0
$6.99

The Amazon Stranger
A perilous trip into the dangerous jungles of Brazil finds the Reel Kids in a struggle with a greedy landowner.
ISBN: 0-927545-83-7
$6.99

The Dangerous Voyage
A mission of mercy to help hurricane victims in Haiti threatens to end in disaster.
ISBN: 0-927545-82-9
$6.99

The Lost Diary
In Turkey, a lost diary means life or death for the Reel Kids and their Turkish host.
ISBN: 0-927545-88-8
$6.99

The Forbidden Road
Dangerous detours await the media club in China on its bike trek from Beijing to the Great Wall.
ISBN: 0-927545-89-6
$6.99

The Danger Zone
Will the Reel Kids' special assignment to war-torn Vietnam end in more hatred and lies?
ISBN: 1-57658-002-4
$6.99

The Himalayan Rescue
Sinister threats and treacherous mountain trails jeopardize the media club's rescue of two orphans in Nepal.
ISBN: 1-57658-027-X
$6.99

Available at your local Christian bookstore or
through YWAM Publishing
1-800-922-2143
www.ywampublishing.com

Also from YWAM Publishing...

Adventure-filled biographies for ages 10 to 100!

Christian Heroes: Then & Now

Gladys Aylward: The Adventure of a Lifetime • 1-57658-019-9
Nate Saint: On a Wing and a Prayer • 1-57658-017-2
Hudson Taylor: Deep in the Heart of China • 1-57658-016-4
Amy Carmichael: Rescuer of Precious Gems • 1-57658-018-0
Eric Liddell: Something Greater Than Gold • 1-57658-137-3
Corrie ten Boom: Keeper of the Angels' Den • 1-57658-136-5
William Carey: Obliged to Go • 1-57658-147-0
George Müller: The Guardian of Bristol's Orphans • 1-57658-145-4
Jim Elliot: One Great Purpose • 1-57658-146-2
Mary Slessor: Forward into Calabar • 1-57658-148-9
David Livingstone: Africa's Trailblazer • 1-57658-153-5
Betty Greene: Wings to Serve • 1-57658-152-7
Adoniram Judson: Bound for Burma • 1-57658-161-6
Cameron Townsend: Good News in Every Language • 1-57658-164-0
Jonathan Goforth: An Open Door in China • 1-57658-174-8
Lottie Moon: Giving Her All for China • 1-57658-188-8
John Williams: Messenger of Peace • 1-57658-256-6
William Booth: Soup, Soap, and Salvation • 1-57658-258-2
Rowland Bingham: Into Africa's Interior • 1-57658-282-5
Ida Scudder: Healing Bodies, Touching Hearts • 1-57658-285-X
Wilfred Grenfell: Fisher of Men • 1-57658-292-2
Lillian Trasher: The Greatest Wonder in Egypt • 1-57658-305-8
Loren Cunningham: Into All the World • 1-57658-199-3
Florence Young: Mission Accomplished • 1-57658-313-9
Sundar Singh: Footprints Over the Mountains • 1-57658-318-X
C.T. Studd: No Retreat • 1-57658-288-4
Rachel Saint: A Star in the Jungle • 1-57658-337-6
Brother Andrew: God's Secret Agent • 1-57658-355-4
Count Zinzendorf: Firstfruit • 1-57658-262-0
Clarence Jones: Mr. Radio • 1-57658-343-0
C.S. Lewis: Master Storyteller • 1-57658-385-6
John Wesley: The World His Parish • 1-57658-382-1

Heroes of History

George Washington Carver: From Slave to Scientist • 1-883002-78-8
Abraham Lincoln: A New Birth of Freedom • 1-883002-79-6
Meriwether Lewis: Off the Edge of the Map • 1-883002-80-X
George Washington: True Patriot • 1-883002-81-8
William Penn: Liberty and Justice for All • 1-883002-82-6
Harriet Tubman: Freedombound • 1-883002-90-7
John Adams: Independence Forever • 1-883002-50-8
Clara Barton: Courage under Fire • 1-883002-51-6
Daniel Boone: Frontiersman • 1-932096-09-4
Theodore Roosevelt: An American Original • 1-932096-10-8
Douglas MacArthur: What Greater Honor • 1-932096-15-9
Benjamin Franklin: Live Wire • 1-932096-14-0
Christopher Columbus: Across the Ocean Sea • 1-932096-23-X
Laura Ingalls Wilder: A Storybook Life • 1-932096-32-9
Thomas Edison: Inspiration and Hard Work • 1-932096-37-X
Alan Shepard: Higher and Faster • 1-93209-641-8

Also available:

Unit Study Curriculum Guides

Turn a great reading experience into an even greater
learning opportunity with a Unit Study Curriculum Guide.
Available for select Christian Heroes: Then & Now
and Heroes of History biographies.

Heroes for Young Readers

Written by Renee Taft Meloche • Illustrated by Bryan Pollard

Introduce younger children to the lives of these heroes
with rhyming text and captivating color illustrations!

All of these series are available from YWAM Publishing
1-800-922-2143 / www.ywampublishing.com